Elizabeth froze, unable to stop listening

"I'm your sister." Abigail's voice came low and angry from behind the oak door. "And I won't stand by and watch you do this. Not this time."

Mark gave an icy laugh that chilled Elizabeth's blood. "Has it ever occurred to you that I might love her?"

"Never in a million years!"

"Do you really believe I'd marry a woman I didn't care for?"

"You're capable of anything," Abigail muttered. "That's why you're going through with this farce! Just like all the others. Only this time you're going to marry her. And you'll kill her, just like you killed...."

"I'm warning you!" Mark said explosively.

Elizabeth stumbled away from the door, her eyes closed on stinging tears. It was not possible. She wouldn't—couldn't—believe it!

Bluebeard's Bride

Sarah Holland

Harlequin Books

TORONTO • NEW YORK • LONDON
AMSTERDAM • PARIS • SYDNEY • HAMBURG
STOCKHOLM • ATHENS • TOKYO • MILAN

Original hardcover edition published in 1985
by Mills & Boon Limited

ISBN 0-373-02705-2

Harlequin Romance first edition July 1985

FOR ALL GORDONIANS
ESPECIALLY
Michael Holland,
Helen Egan,
Simon King,
Allan, and Scarlet Party.

CHAPTER ONE

IT was too dark, too still. The silence on the Essex country road was eerie, and she glanced away from the main beam of her headlights to see dark shadows forming on either side in the hedgerows. She had always hated the long, lonely drive to her sister's house, but tonight she hated it more than ever, because that long black limousine had been following her ever since she'd left London.

At first she had shrugged it off as coincidence, but now as she flicked her violet eyes to the rear-view mirror, she felt the hairs on the back of her neck stand on end. Without thinking, she clicked the lock on her door down, and frowned, realising that that one action made the whole thing even more frightening. She had just acknowledged the fact that she was being followed.

Slowing to take a tight bend, she noticed a junction to her left, and hoped the car would turn off. But as the road straightened out again she saw the gleaming yellow eyes of the limousine slide along behind her again, and her heart began to beat faster. Her sister's house was still a good ten minutes' drive from here. The thought of the warm, inviting house cheered her up a little, and she hoped there would be as many people there as usual. Melanie had so many friends, and the big old house they had shared as children was always packed at the weekends with musicians and writers, all lounging around on the fat comfortable settees that were falling to pieces.

A solitary street-lamp glowed up ahead, and she felt relief flood over her. Driving towards it, she indicated left, and slowed at the white lines. The sinister, ever-present nose of the limousine waited silently behind her. Elizabeth felt a jolt of panic, and tried to pull away too fast. The car stalled. Pulses leaping, she fumbled with the key. It wouldn't start. Glancing quickly in the mirror, she tried again. The engine burst into life, and she pulled away with a screech of tyres, the wheels almost slipping on the sloping road.

She was in darkness again, save for the white beam of her headlights, and the glare of the limousine behind her. Why on earth should anyone want to follow me? she thought, slamming the gearstick, driving faster than ever. Especially someone rich enough to drive a limousine. She was just another struggling young singer, living on the small inheritance from her parents' death two years ago. Soon, the money would run out and she would have to get a proper job. But in the meantime she was trying to fulfil a dream she and her sister had shared since childhood. Melanie had started picking out tunes on their dusty old piano on rainy days, and soon Elizabeth had been singing with her while she played. Now Melanie spent her time writing songs which she passed on to Elizabeth to sing. There was no basic difference between those quiet afternoons spent in the front room, and the afternoons now, spent in their makeshift recording studio.

The engine began to splutter unhealthily, and Elizabeth jolted back to the present. Frowning, she pressed her foot heavily on the accelerator. The engine coughed in protest, and Elizabeth saw a light flash on on the decrepit dashboard.

She was running out of petrol. Not now, she thought desperately, please not now. At times like this she usually tried being nice to her ancient car, calling it pet names and soothing it back into life. But charm wouldn't work right now. This was no temperamental fault on the part of her car—it was her fault for not stopping at that petrol station three miles back. She'd been too concerned with the car following her to notice the gauge.

With one last splutter, the car ground to a halt. Elizabeth felt her heart begin to bound around in her chest as the limousine stopped too. She swallowed, watching it stop behind her. The yellow eyes of its headlamps closed, plunging her into darkness. Quickly she dived over to the passenger door and locked it, winding up her window frantically.

Then she just sat tight, refusing to move. Nothing moved, there was no sound. All she could hear was her own frightened breathing. For all she knew, a rich maniac was sitting right behind her, and the thought made her shiver with icy fear, her pulses hammering at her wrist and throat.

A sound made her jump, hands gripping the useless wheel, hands which she now realised were slippery with perspiration. The long black door of the limousine had swung open and someone was getting out.

Heavy male feet crunched on the gravel road, and Elizabeth closed her eyes tight. Opening them a little as the footsteps stopped, she saw a face at the window, and felt her heart hammer painfully. Knuckles rapped on the glass, and she was suddenly overwhelmed by a flood of fear caused by darkness and isolation. He rapped again.

Slowly Elizabeth turned her head. The man was big, solidly built, like a boxer, with a smooth bullet-shaped head, little piggy eyes watching her from beneath a peaked cap. He didn't look harmless. But then again, he didn't look dangerous.

He made winding motions with one sausage-fingered hand, and Elizabeth wound her window down half an inch, her hands shaking.

'Mr Blackthorne thought you might need some help,' he said, and his voice was surprisingly soft, making him seem more sinister than ever.

Dry-mouthed, Elizabeth asked, 'Who's Mr Blackthorne?'

The man watched her for a second with expressionless eyes, then turned and walked back to the car behind. She watched his solid retreat in her wing mirror. He bent his head to the rear door and there was a smooth whirr as an electric window rolled down. Words were exchanged in the darkness, then the rear door swung open.

A pair of long legs stepped out, followed by a tall body uncoiling with panther-like grace. Elizabeth saw the ripple of muscle beneath the black evening suit, the tanned skin exposed at throat and wrist. Then she saw his face, a stark powerful silhouette.

Blue eyes glittered beneath hooded lids and winged black brows. Raven-black hair blew back from his forehead and he raked it down with a shadowy hand before coming towards her, his lean body glimmering in the patchy wing mirror.

'Good evening.' His voice was deep and drawling, and she looked round in surprise to see him watching her with an amused expression. 'I take it you've run out of petrol?'

Elizabeth nodded slowly. He was devastatingly attractive at such close quarters, and she felt her fear ebbing away immediately. He was smiling at her, his teeth white against his tan.

'No problem.' He moved to open the door, but found it locked, and looked back at her with a patient expression. Elizabeth looked at the long fingers which rested on the mottled chrome door handle, and suddenly felt foolish for being so afraid.

He was still waiting for her to open the door and she smiled slightly as she unlocked it. 'Sorry,' she started to unfasten her seat-belt, her fingers clumsy under that blue gaze, 'but I expected . . .' she broke off, about to say she had expected someone rather more frightening, and flushed, realised he had read her thoughts.

'What?' he said lazily. 'A two-headed monster?'

Elizabeth dropped her eyes, her dark lashes sweeping her cheeks. 'Something of that sort,' she agreed, her cheeks dimpling.

He held out one hand to help her out of the car. 'Sorry to disappoint you!' he drawled, and she laughed. He slid his hands in his pockets, eyeing her. 'Come over here. Crane will put some petrol in the tank for you.'

She followed him as he walked lazily over to the limousine. 'Do you have enough?'

He shot her a wry look over one shoulder. 'I'm not going to syphon it, if that's what you mean.' He lounged casually against the shiny black car, taking a cigarette out of his inside jacket pocket and lighting it with a slim silver lighter. Tendrils of grey smoke wreathed around his handsome face as he inhaled.

Elizabeth watched the chauffeur take a dull white can of petrol out of the boot and walk stolidly over to her car, unscrewing the petrol cap and pouring it in with an audible glugging sound.

'Where are you travelling to?' asked the stranger, and she turned back to look at him, huddling into her sheepskin coat a little as the wind blew across the fields.

'Mayfield. Do you know it?'

He nodded. 'Yes. Pretty little village.' He watched her push her hands deeper into the sheepskin coat, and tilted his head to one side. 'If you're cold we can sit in the car.'

Elizabeth felt an answering smile tug at her lips. 'Got a good heater, has it?'

His eyes glittered. 'Excellent,' he drawled, and swung the door open in a swift movement, standing tall and dark watching her. She hesitated, remembering that he had been following her. Had it just been coincidence? she wondered, frowning.

He studied her with lazy amusement. 'I'm not going to attack you, if that's what's worrying you,' he said drily, and she flushed, feeling rather silly.

'Of course not!' There was no reason for her to think he would. He was obviously wealthy and very attractive. She got into the rear of the car, feeling pressurised, which in turn made her feel uneasy.

He slid in beside her. 'Do you live in Mayfield?' he asked casually, and she watched him start to close the door.

'Yes,' she lied, then wondered why on earth she had done it.

Then she knew. He stopped, his hand freezing

on the door handle, leaving it slightly ajar. Elizabeth watched his face shutter, blinking once, the black lashes flickering against his tanned cheek.

'Oh?' He didn't turn his head or move, and she felt suddenly uneasy.

'I've been visiting friends in London,' she said slowly, watching him. There was something very odd about all this.

He closed the door with a cool movement, and turned to look at her, blue eyes hidden by those hooded lids. Then he smiled, but it didn't make her relax the way it had done before. There was no charm in this smile, it was controlled, deliberate, his white teeth glinting in the dark interior of the car.

'So have I,' he said, as though trying to change the subject, 'I'm on my way to Carthax. It's not far from Mayfield.'

'Oh,' she said politely, and was relieved to see Crane coming back with the now empty can of petrol. He went round and opened the boot, putting it away again.

Elizabeth turned to the stranger with a smile. 'How much do I owe you?' She started to fish in her jeans pocket for some crumpled pound notes.

He waved the money away with a long hand. 'Forget it,' he drawled, opening the door again and stepping out while she clambered out after him, relieved that she could go. She wouldn't feel entirely safe until she was at Melanie's.

'Please,' she offered him the money again as they walked back to her car, 'I'm very grateful.'

He observed her with wry amusement. 'It won't break my bank,' he told her, watching as she opened her door and stood waiting to get in.

'Well,' she smiled, 'thanks again. It was really very kind of you.'

He nodded and stood back as she began to get in, but at that moment Crane suddenly started coming towards them quickly, waving something metallic in his hand.

'Sir,' he called out, 'I forgot to put Miss Wyatt's cap back.'

Elizabeth's heart stopped.

The stranger shot a vicious look at Crane, who froze, whitening.

Elizabeth fumbled with the ignition key frantically. Revving the engine, she slammed the car into gear and almost knocked the stranger down as she screeched away into the night, her door swinging open.

'You stupid bastard!' The biting tone of his voice rang in her ears as she roared away, looking in the rear-view mirror, seeing him staring after her like a threatening shadow, watching her red tail lights disappear round the corner.

So she'd been right!' How else could the chauffeur have known her name? She had never even mentioned it—neither had he. All she knew about him was that his surname was Blackthorne, and the name hovered on the tip of her tongue like a distant memory. Where had she heard it before? Who was he? And what did he do?

But why on earth was he interested in her? She drove faster than ever, watching her mirror with one eye and refusing to slow down until she got to Mayfield. At least he hadn't followed her—that much she had to be grateful for.

She hoped to God she never saw him again.

Jeremy answered the door. 'Oh, hullo,' he said

indifferently, turning at once to go back into the warm front room where the yellow lights glowed through the ragged curtains.

Elizabeth closed the door behind her and slid her coat off. She watched Jeremy's departing back and heard the sound of the television as she opened the peeling white door.

'Who was it?' asked a male voice with casual interest as he went in.

'Liz,' replied Jeremy, sitting on a fat green sofa and turning his blond head as Elizabeth came in.

A few faces turned in her direction and smiled, then looked back at the flickering television screen. Elizabeth picked her way across the room, feeling grateful for the normal bored atmosphere, It's nice to be somewhere normal and boring, she thought, and laughed under her breath.

At that moment Melanie came in, black hair swinging in a glossy bell around her face. 'Oh, hi!' she said, noticing Elizabeth across the room. 'How long have you been here?'

'Ten seconds,' said Jeremy, one eye on the television.

Somebody kicked the door shut, grumbling about letting the heat out, and Melanie raised her brows with sympathy. Elizabeth bit her lip, wondering whether she ought to tell anyone about what had happened on her way here. She didn't expect the man to turn up at any minute knocking on her door, but she was still worried about it.

Melanie was smiling at her. 'Good trip down?'

Elizabeth hesitated. 'I ran out of petrol,' she said slowly, and unbuttoned her creamy wool cardigan because the fire was so hot. 'Why do you have to have that turned up so high?' she asked, looking at the flickering blue-gold flames of the gas fire.

'Because we're troglodytes,' said Jeremy, looking like a buttercup pixie with his pale blond brows almost invisible, cornflower blue eyes watching her beneath a silky blond fringe.

'Did you have to walk to a garage?' asked Melanie.

Elizabeth shook her head. 'No.' She paused, wondering how to phrase it. 'Someone stopped and gave me a spare gallon.' Which was as brief as it could get. But then what would they think if she told them a limousine had followed her all the way from London? That she was going paranoid? She shifted uncomfortably in her seat. *Was* she going paranoid?

'Lucky old you!' Melanie laughed, and lit a cigarette, aiming the spent match at an ashtray across the room. Unfortunately, her aim was not perfect and it bounced off the edge and fell on the floor. 'Missed!' she said with disgust as Elizabeth bent to pick it up. 'By the way, the piano's free if you want to practise your vocals.'

Elizabeth looked up. 'I've done all my exercises today.' She always did. She practised her scales three times a day, refusing to miss a single session, even if she was ill. Missing even one meant her voice weakened slightly, and it took another day to get back into peak condition, and to a singer, that was a day wasted. In that day she could have been pushing her voice higher, further.

'Nicky brought the drum machine down,' Melanie told her. 'We can start work on the new song tomorrow. Even Jeremy's offered to help.'

All eyes turned to Jeremy.

'What?' he protested. 'It's a dirty lie!'

Elizabeth sat back, allowing the conversation to drift lazily over her head. They'd been waiting for the drum machine for two weeks. Nicky had taken his time bringing it—but then it was so expensive to hire one of the damned things. And Mr Roache next door complained bitterly when they brought in a real drummer and drum kit because it was so noisy. Elizabeth sighed. It would be nice to own a drum computer—but there just wasn't enough money. They cost thousands, and Elizabeth was not exactly made of money.

The mysterious Mr Blackthorne popped unbidden into her head, and she frowned, wondering whether he had really been following her. It seemed inconceivable. Yet his chauffeur had known her name.

Frowning, she looked across at Nicky, who sat on the other side of the room playing backgammon—and winning. Nicky always won. He was the sort of person who wanted badly to win—and people like that generally got what they wanted, because they had the edge on their opponents.

He had been her manager for a year now—hers and Jeremy's. He had whirled into their lives like a hurricane, albeit a likeable hurricane. Adept at organisation, he had picked them both up from their amateur careers and threaded them together, creating order out of chaos. Elizabeth didn't know whether either she or Jeremy would ever be succesful—but she knew they stood a good chance with Nicky Henderson behind them.

Somebody prodded her, and she looked round in surprise to see a red dice being placed in her hand.

'We're rolling for coffee,' Melanie explained, and threw her dice along with the others as they all craned forward to see who lost.

Elizabeth threw a one.

'That's not fair!' she protested amidst hoots of laughter.

'No getting out of it!' said Jeremy, laughing. 'Into the kitchen you go.' He handed her a grimy white mug. 'Two sugars!'

Elizabeth collected the other cups and went out, closing the door with one foot. The little kitchen was cold, one window pane cracked right across, and she felt the icy November air sting her cheeks. Going over to it, she pulled the curtains shut and switched the kettle on.

The front room door opened and she heard footsteps approach just as she was looking in the bare fridge unsuccessfully for a pint of milk.

'Looking for milk?' Nicky came into the kitchen, and pointed to the run-down cupboard where a lone pint of milk stood on a shelf next to an old packet of dry, cracked spaghetti.

'Thanks.' She waited for the kettle to boil, glancing at him wryly. 'Sorry about last week's vocals. They weren't exactly up to scratch, were they?'

He shrugged. 'It doesn't matter. We all have our off days.'

Elizabeth smiled. 'I seem to have more than my fair share.'

'I'd be a fool if I expected you to be as reliable as that drum computer,' drawled Nicky, and his dark eyes flicked over her with amusement. 'Although I'm sometimes tempted to find the right buttons and press them.' He laughed under his breath as she looked away, colour stinging her cheeks. There had always been an attraction between them, running under the surface. She wondered if it had more to do with his looks than anything else. Tall, well-built and black-haired, he fitted neatly into her idea of the perfect man. But his personality was too out of key with hers for a permanent relationship, and that, in effect, was the only relationship she would consider with any man.

Nicky was watching her shrewdly. 'But don't worry about it,' he said, using a more neutral tone. 'There's no rush. I'm not planning on showing those demo tapes to any record companies for at least four months.'

Elizabeth nodded, spooning coffee into mugs. She eyed him. 'Are you going to help, or just lean there and look decorative?'

He gave her a crooked grin. 'Just lean.' Folding his arms and crossing his long legs, he did just that, the denim of his jeans scuffing the floor. 'Actually, I wanted to talk to you about something.'

'Oh?' She looked up, the bright white centre light picking out strands of midnight blue in her hair, making her face look like an oil painting with those fine black brows and lashes, stark violet eyes all set in a pale face.

'Are you busy tomorrow night?' he asked. 'Because I want to take you to a party—a big party. Lots of money on two legs.'

'Anyone I know?' Elizabeth picked up the kettle, feeling the steam condense on her hand.

'You may have heard of him. Mark Blackthorne.'

Elizabeth dropped the spoon, and it clattered on to the peeling formica table as she remembered the solidly built chauffeur bending to her window and saying softly, 'Mr Blackthorne thought you might need some help.' And of course she had replied, 'Who's Mr Blackthorne?' But even as she remembered doing it she felt a flicker of a memory in the back of her mind, like someone's name on the tip of her tongue, and she was caught up in the frustration of trying to remember where she had heard his name before.

'I take it you *have* heard of him,' Nicky said drily, 'and I appreciate your appreciation. This guy's got a finger in so many pies he makes Little Jack Horner look like an amateur.'

Elizabeth stared at him, and felt a prickle of that uneasiness return to her. It was all too pat, too convenient. And it was all happening too fast. Coincidence? She dismissed that idea with a slight shake of her head. How on earth could you put this lot down to coincidence? Someone called Blackthorne had followed her tonight, followed her for miles from London to Essex, when he should have overtaken her in that fast shiny limousine. Her car couldn't even stretch comfortably to fifty miles an hour without rattling and humming dangerously. His car ought to have flown straight over her head at a hundred miles an hour—but he had stayed behind her every inch of the way. And he had known her name.

'Liz?' Nicky was frowning. 'Are you okay? You've gone quite pale.'

She smiled, giving a little sigh and turning to look at him. 'I don't know, Nicky. I think I met him tonight, on the road—when I ran out of petrol.'

Nicky looked puzzled. 'He told you who he was?'

'Sort of.' She bit her lip, trying to ignore the gut feeling in the pit of her stomach that told her she was right, Mark Blackthorne had been following her, and he was laying a trap even now as she spoke to Nicky in the little white kitchen. 'But that's only half of it. Nicky ... I think he was following me. All the way from London.'

Nicky's dark brows jerked together in disbelief, then he gave an uncertain laugh. 'Sure! The guy's a lonely little fruitcake, everyone knows that.' He shook his head as Elizabeth began to protest. 'Come on, Liz, this is Mark Blackthorne we're talking about. And I can assure you that this is one guy with every single marble right in place.'

She caught hold of his arms. 'I'm serious, Nicky!' She had his attention then, he was looking at her in surprise. It wasn't often that she forced a point like this. 'He was behind me from the minute I left my flat. I couldn't mistake it—he was in a limousine. When I ran out of petrol he stopped, but there was something really odd about it.'

Nicky studied her seriously. 'You can say that again! Men like Blackthorne don't make a habit of following poverty-stricken girls around. He usually does his shopping among beauty queens and film stars.' He gave her an affectionate smile. 'No offence, Liz, but ...'

'Yes, I know,' she smiled too, 'I know. But—' She shook her head, feeling very confused. Nicky was right, it just did not add up. 'Like I said— it seemed odd at the time.'

Nicky was studying her, his head tilted to one side. 'Does this mean you don't want to come? It's a great opportunity to meet people who matter—but I'll understand, of course, if you decide not to.'

Elizabeth looked at him, thinking hard. If she was right, and Mark Blackthorne was playing an intricate and inexplicable game, then it made sense to keep well away from him.

She took a deep breath. 'He knew my name, Nicky.'

His frown deepened. 'What?'

She pushed her hands into her jeans pockets and sighed, leaning against the cupboard. 'I wasn't going to tell you, because I don't actually want to be right. But his chauffeur knew my name, and I certainly didn't tell him. I didn't even tell Blackthorne—why should I tell the chauffeur?'

Nicky pursed his lips, perplexed. 'He could have seen it when he was filling the tank up.'

'Really?' Her voice was dry. 'Where? In neon lights on the back window? Come off it, Nicky!'

He was silent, thinking this over. Elizabeth sighed, going over to the kettle and pouring out boiling water into all the cups. She stirred milk in, distracted. For some reason, she was curious to know exactly why Mark Blackthorne had been following her, why he had known her name. There was just no logic to it, for heaven's sake. Nothing added up, and the endless puzzle in her head was irritating her.

Nicky looked across at her. 'So you're not coming?'

She shook her head. 'You go. Report back to me—if anything seems in the least bit odd, let me know.'

Nicky slid his hands in his denim pockets. 'You're the boss,' he said, eyes amused. Then he stopped, his face serious. 'I'm not trying to force you to come, but . . .'

'But?' she enquired drily.

He laughed. 'Well, if I were in your shoes, I'd feel a lot safer going to the party, to be frank. You'll be with me, so you'll be quite safe, and at least you'll be able to find out what he's up to.'

She shot a look at him. 'That had occurred to me.'

'Why not do it, then?' Nicky raised dark brows. 'He can't eat you. And you can see for yourself what sort of man he is.'

Elizabeth felt her eyes narrow. 'Why should I want to do that?'

Nicky assumed his superior smile. 'I can't think of any other reason why he should know your name or follow you. He must fancy you.'

He turned and began to walk out of the room, leaving Elizabeth staring after him. Slowly she started to put the mugs on a red tin tray, her mind distracted. Mark Blackthorne? Fancy her? How ridiculous, she thought slowly. But why else would he follow her?

There was no answer to the puzzle. She had no choice but to go to the party and find out. Otherwise he might very well come looking for her, and what would she do then?

'Nicky!' she called out, and he came back into the kitchen a few seconds later.

'What?' His eyes fell on the tray. 'Need some help?'

She shook her head. 'I've changed my mind. I'll come tomorrow.'

Nicky smiled, ruffling her black hair. 'That's more like it. *Courage, mon brave!*'

Elizabeth returned his smile, but felt her nerves begin to tighten in anticipation. What would she do if Mark Blackthorne did 'fancy her', as Nicky so delicately put it? He didn't look like the sort of man who was after a permanent relationship!

Her mouth thinned unhappily. She knew only too well what was on Mark Blackthorne's mind if what Nicky said was true. And Elizabeth was not interested. For one thing, she didn't have the time to spare for passionate love affairs with wealthy men, and she wasn't in the market for the odd diamond bracelet or fur coat. She had better things to do with her time.

Nicky glanced at her and did a double-take. 'What a face!' he said with wicked delight, laughing. 'I wouldn't want to be Blackthorne tomorrow night!'

Elizabeth gave him a cross look. 'Well, how would you feel?'

Nicky eyed her drily. 'I'm afraid I've never been in the same position,' he drawled.

Elizabeth smiled grudgingly. 'No.' Men were never put in this sort of situation. Which was why, no doubt, they were only too happy to impose themselves on women. We're such poor little helpless creatures, Elizabeth thought irritably, with nothing on our minds except who our next boy-friend will be.

But Mark Blackthorne had picked the wrong girl for that sort of treatment. Elizabeth would not consider putting her career in jeopardy for any man. Unless, of course, she fell hopelessly in love. But she had met Mark Blackthorne, and she knew he was definitely Mr Wrong.

A very attractive Mr Wrong, she had to admit. But no shining Prince in silver armour, even so.

CHAPTER TWO

THEY were up early the next day, going into the front room to wake up everyone who had slept on the three large sofas. Elizabeth carried in a red tin tray of coffee while bodies groaned, squinting against the assault of bright sunlight and huddling back into their quilts.

'Rise and shine!' called Melanie with wicked relish, flinging the ragged curtains back with a flourish. 'Heavens! Not tired still?'

Jeremy peered across at Elizabeth. 'Is this necessary?' he mumbled, accepting the coffee she gave him and putting it on the carpet next to his makeshift bed.

' 'Fraid so,' Elizabeth grinned at him, and he made a face, huddling back into the pretty flowered quilt, his fair hair ruffled and untidy. 'We've got work to do,' she told him, amused.

Jeremy ran a hand jerkily over his eyes, the pale lashes sticking together. 'Don't talk to me about work!'

'Shut up, Dracula.' Nicky's voice came from the doorway, and she looked over her shoulder to see him looking disgustingly fresh and clean in pale blue denims and a white shirt, his dark hair clean from a shower. 'And get out of your coffin!' He raised his brows at Elizabeth. 'You lot can get this room tidied up. I'm laying down the drum track, so stay out of my way for the next couple of hours. I don't want to be disturbed.' He left the room briskly.

Melanie put her hands on her slim hips. 'Anyone would think it was his house!' she complained.

Nevertheless, no one dared defy him, and they rounded up all available hands to clear the room, emptying overflowing ashtrays into plastic bags, polishing everything, Hoovering everything. When they had finished it looked like a new room, sparkling from top to bottom.

Jeremy stood back leaning on his broom in amazement. 'It looks like somebody's house!' he exclaimed, staggered.

In the afternoon, Elizabeth went into the back room to add the vocals. Standing among black leads, headphones clamped to her ears, she sang into the expensive Sennheiser microphone with her eyes closed.

Nicky was operating the sixteen-track recording desk while Jeremy sat listening on the floor, hands behind his head, smiling. It took half an hour for her voice to warm up properly, but it was worth the wait. Today she was on top form, and cleared all the pitfalls in the song with ease.

As her voice soared in clear high tones, Elizabeth felt the excitement rise in her, controlling the voice, phrasing each word like an arrow, getting perfect tone on the vowels, concise feeling on the consonants.

The last few bars drifted away, and Nicky switched off the tape. Elizabeth opened her eyes.

'Beautiful,' Nicky said quietly.

Elizabeth beamed proudly—she couldn't help it.

Jeremy sighed, and stretched. 'Yep. You're definitely going to be a star, Liz.'

Elizabeth tried not to smile too brightly.

'Nonsense!' she said, but wanted to dance around the room, although she restrained herself with admirable control.

Nicky was watching her with an indulgent smile. 'It isn't fair, you know. Most singers would give their right arms to have your range.'

Jeremy shook his head, sighing. 'Three octaves!' he exclaimed. 'Three! I've only got one and a half!'

Nicky rewound the tape. 'And the song's perfect for you. Nice powerful ballad, plenty of room to let the voice come out.'

Elizabeth nodded, feeling on top of the world. 'I really love singing it. Especially the long high notes at the end. All the power comes soaring out.'

Nicky watched her, smiling. 'You've come a long way since I first heard you.' He glanced at his watch casually, then back at her. 'And you'll go even further if you get dressed for that party! Plenty of people there who can help you.'

Elizabeth went upstairs a moment later, taking the steps two at a time. It gave her such an exhilarating rush to sing well. On a good day, she felt as though she could fly on top of her voice. On a bad day, she felt hurt and depressed—but determined to get back into top form.

Lying in the cracked bathtub later, she knew she would never be able to give this up, not for any man. No man had ever been able to make her feel as excited, happy and full as singing did. Is that how being in love feels? she wondered, frowning. Feeling as though you could dance on air, smiling like an idiot? Soaping her arms, she thought of Mark Blackthorne.

Cruel blue eyes, winged black brows and a face

that contained harsh power leapt into her mind. Shivering, she slid further into the hot water, goosebumps breaking out on her breasts. He was a man to fear, not fall in love with. He would never make her feel the way her voice did. Just the thought of him made her stomach tighten with fear.

Tonight needed something special. Elizabeth had the very thing—a long white silk dress that left her shoulders bare, the bodice resting just above her breasts with no straps. A pair of long white gloves completed the picture of cool innocence.

In her bedroom, she imagined her meeting with Mark Blackthorne. How dared he frighten her like that? How dared he think she would leap into bed with him for the price of a diamond bracelet? She would teach him a lesson! She would be cool, controlled, very much a lady—and a lady who was not interested.

Piling her black hair in curly disarray on her head, she clasped a thick gold necklace around her throat, coiled like a gleaming snake. Spraying on Joy perfume, she looked in the mirror. A cool, elegant lady stared back at her. Not the casual young girl in jeans and a sweater he had met last night. She smiled to herself, imagining his face.

They drove to the party in Nicky's Capri. Elizabeth had borrowed Melanie's silver fox fur jacket, and lifted her head above the soft fur collar as they drove through Essex. She was nervous still, very nervous. Mark Blackthorne was a dark and frightening man. But she refused to be intimidated by him.

Carthax House loomed before them like a haunted Victorian castle. Dark turrets pierced the moonlit night, a blue-white light shone over the huge double doors, the air condensing in a fine mist beneath the heat of the light. A cavalcade of expensive cars glittered along the gravel drive. The acres of land around it were well-manicured lawns bordered by spiky threatening trees.

'Creepy!' Jeremy poked his head between the seats to stare at it.

Elizabeth stared silently at the menacing spikes of the turrets. Nicky parked the car and they went to the tall central doors, while Jeremy lingered to look admiringly through the window of a black Porsche.

The door was answered by a tall man with white hair who glanced at their invitations wordlessly and led them in.

The huge stone room they went into was filled with wealthy guests who moved around the ancient floor like gossamer silk, diamonds flashing at their throats like frost, the men in black dinner suits. A huge chandelier glittered with crystal and gold, oil paintings hung on the cold stone walls, the polished floor was scattered with thick silk rugs. Mahogany furniture gleamed under the weight of antique silver. A minstrels' gallery ran along the back with an orchestra inside it, a tapestry draped over the wooden ledge.

'Good evening.' The deep drawling voice made her spin, eyes flying to his face.

Mark Blackthorne was watching her intently, the cruel blue eyes narrowed on her face. Elizabeth stared at him in stunned silence. The man must walk like a cat, she thought. She hadn't heard anyone approach.

'Welcome to my home,' he said softly, eyes piercing hers, and she felt herself nod jerkily in silent reply, staring at him.

A cool smile touched his hard mouth and he turned to look at Nicky. 'Mr Henderson—delighted you could come. I take it these are your two protégés?'

Nicky leapt into enthusiastic reply, while Elizabeth stood in silence, listening to him introduce first Jeremy, then herself, but she only stood and stared as Mark Blackthorne turned slowly to her, taking her smooth white-gloved hand in his.

'Miss Wyatt,' he murmured, brushing his mouth across her wrist, his lips burning the pale flesh exposed by the buttons of the glove.

'How nice to meet you,' she said coldly. 'Your face seems so familiar.'

His eyes glittered beneath the bright chandelier. Cool amusement made him smile again as he turned to Nicky. 'There are some people from R.C.I. here—you might find them useful.' He nodded to a group of men in the corner, their faces flushed from champagne, a sharp-faced beauty adorning each of their arms.

Nicky shot a quick look in their direction, eyes gleaming with ambition. 'Great! Come on, you two, let's introduce ourselves!'

But Mark Blackthorne's long fingers curled over Elizabeth's arm and she looked at him in alarm, her eyes wide. 'I'll take care of Miss Wyatt,' he drawled coolly.

Nicky wasn't sure how to handle this. 'Oh,' he said, looking from one to the other, shifting his weight uncertainly. He didn't want to offend Mark Blackthorne any more than he wanted to upset Elizabeth.

'Run along, Henderson.' Mark's voice was a cynical drawl. He understood Nicky only too well. 'She'll be quite safe with me.'

Nicky looked worriedly at Elizabeth. 'If you're sure . . .' he said as Elizabeth stared in disbelief, watching him walk away with Jeremy, who was whispering excitedly in his ear.

Elizabeth looked angrily at Mark Blackthorne. 'Very deft!' she snapped hotly.

He gave her a cool smile. 'Thank you,' he drawled, watching her mouth tighten with irritation.

'Why did you do that?' she asked, her heart beating fast with nerves and anger as she struggled to look cool and confident.

'I want to talk to you.'

'Don't you think you should have asked me first?'

The winged black brows rose. 'Would you have agreed?'

Her eyes flashed. 'I seriously doubt it.' She looked pointedly at the long hard fingers curled around her arm. 'And I don't agree now. Please take your hand off my arm!'

He tightened his grip, his eyes glittering. 'Admirable spirit,' he drawled.

She glared at him. 'Don't patronise me!'

'Oh, I never patronise a lady,' he said softly, his voice chilling. 'Especially one so beautiful.' The blue eyes raked her slowly from head to foot, lingering on the soft white skin of her bare shoulders, the swell of her breasts beneath the white silk.

Hot colour stung her cheeks, and she tried to pull her arm discreetly out of his grip. She didn't want to attract the attention of the other guests.

Mark's fingers bit into her arm. 'The gloves are enchanting,' he drawled smokily, eyes hooded. 'Totally covered from head to foot.' His other hand came up slowly to run long fingers over her bare skin. 'Except for naked shoulders. Very exciting!'

Elizabeth shivered, goosebumps breaking out on her bare shoulders. 'Stop it!' she said heatedly, brushing his hand away as his fingers slid to the skin just above her breasts.

Mark smiled slowly. 'I come as the hunter to find I'm the prey.'

'Don't be so pompous!' she snapped.

He stared at her in surprise.

Elizabeth pulled her arm away successfully, rubbing it. 'You sound like Sir Jasper!' she said angrily.

He stared in silence, then started to laugh, and she watched in surprise to see the menace leave his face, and charm take its place.

'Is that how I seem?' he asked, smiling. 'I'll have to watch myself in future.'

Elizabeth refused to let her guard down. Eyeing him suspiciously, she said, 'I thought you wanted to talk?'

The smile left his face, and he shook his head. 'Not here—it's too crowded.' Watching her from beneath hooded lids, he said, 'Shall we go somewhere more private?'

Before she could reply, he placed one strong hand on her back and began to propel her forward. They walked across the baronial hall, she in her virginal white dress, he in his dark evening suit, a red carnation in his lapel. She glanced at him through her lashes as they walked side by side. He was devastatingly attractive; that hard-boned face would have been enough on its own, but his body was lean and powerful, rippling muscle exuding animal sexuality and danger.

People stared as they passed. Female eyes watched Mark Blackthorne with a mixture of fear and excitement, and Elizabeth understood that reaction. She felt it too—felt it as she walked next to him, her mouth dry with it. It was an unconscious, unstoppable force; everything about him spelt power, masculinity, sexuality—and danger. To see him walking across the room was to feel the instant impact of primeval attraction.

But he was not the only subject of their stares. Elizabeth felt her skin chill as their eyes followed her, as though she was a ghost floating along before them. She lifted her head, ignoring them.

They went into a corridor outside the hall, and Mark walked ahead, pushing open an oak door and ushering her inside.

She found herself in an intimate Victorian study, with a fire leaping and spitting in the grate, lighting the dark red walls with flickering shadows, long red velvet curtains falling at the window, a dark mahogany desk in one corner and a solid leather couch by the fire.

'Brandy?' Mark closed the door, leaning against it.

Elizabeth looked over her shoulder to see him watching her with his dark head tilted back, his eyes indeed those of a hunter. She shivered in unconscious reaction.

'Please.' Looking away, she felt wary. In this small silent room his presence was even more disturbing. Potent masculinity was all very well in small doses, but Mark Blackthorne was far too much for one woman to cope with all on her own. Especially me, she thought as she went to the fire and sat down on the burgundy couch. Elizabeth had very little experience of men. All her life since discovering her voice had been spent in carefree, single-minded pursuit of the perfect song to match it. Men had never entered more than the periphery of her day-to-day life.

Mark came over to the couch cupping two brandy glasses, one of which he handed to her. Her eyes focused on the large, strong hand around the glass, and she shivered.

'Why were you following me last night?' she asked suddenly, trying to take her attention from his physical presence.

It didn't work. He sat down slowly beside her, and her heart beat too fast as she watched him stretch out those long legs, raising one powerful arm to rest along the back of the couch, his hand almost touching her shoulder.

'I saw you at the Cartouche a few weeks ago,' he said simply.

Elizabeth remembered the occasion—the Cartouche was a Mayfair nightclub frequented by stars, important people and 'money', as Nicky called it. Elizabeth had gone along to a party held for the launch of a film, and had only been invited because Nicky knew the man who had written the soundtrack and theme song.

She studied Mark. 'I don't remember you.' She knew she would never have forgotten him if they'd met. He was not the forgettable type.

'No,' he drawled softly, 'but I remember you.'

Her mouth went dry at the predatory look in his eyes. 'We weren't introduced.' She felt sure of that.

He inclined his black head. 'True. You left a few moments after I arrived. I saw you across the room.'

'But why follow me?' she asked in an undertone.

He was silent for a moment, considering her through sooty black lashes. Then one dark brow rose very slowly. 'Love at first sight?' he said softly.

Elizabeth laughed, but her heart skipped a beat and she clutched her brandy tightly. 'Don't be silly!' she said huskily.

Mark took a cigarette from an antique silver box on the mahogany table beside him. 'I saw you driving along Park Lane last night.' He flicked a silver lighter, the flame at the tip of the cigarette, his blue eyes watching her steadily. 'I just decided to follow you.'

She shot him a look of disbelief. 'Just like that?'

'Just like that,' he said smokily, and drew on the cigarette, smoke curling around his dark face.

'Why?' Elizabeth watched him tensely.

His gaze grew suddenly intense. 'My dear,' he murmured, and his hand moved fractionally, allowing one long finger to run from her shoulder to her neck, 'you're very beautiful.'

Her pulses leapt under that stare. She made no move to brush his hands away, and she knew why. She liked his touch far too much.

Their eyes held for several seconds. Her mouth went dry. 'What did you intend to do?' she asked through dry lips.

He considered her coolly. 'Get to know you. Ask you to dinner.' He shrugged and she saw the muscle ripple beneath the black jacket, 'God knows—anything. I hadn't thought that far ahead, to tell the truth.'

'And when I broke down?'

'Ah . . .' he said softly, eyes glittering in the firelight, 'well, that was a little unexpected. It rather threw me.'

Elizabeth nodded. 'That's why you didn't get out of the car at first.'

'Exactly.' He studied her shrewdly. 'Were you frightened, last night?'

She nodded again. 'Yes,' she said under her breath.

Mark's hard mouth parted as he watched her intensely. 'And now?' he asked in a voice so soft it made her lean forward fractionally.

'I'm not sure.'

The long fingers resting on her bare throat moved slowly, sliding to her chin with seductive touch. 'You must be sure,' he murmured, his lids half open.

Elizabeth swallowed, her eyes falling against her will to rest on his hard mouth, knowing she wanted to feel it move on hers. Her heart was beating much too fast, and she knew she was in the hands of an expert seducer, but she couldn't bear to stop the delicious sensations that his touch caused. It was ridiculous. She'd only known him for ten minutes, and she was startled to realise she was already falling under his spell.

She tried to move away. 'I must get back to the party,' she said huskily. 'Nicky will wonder where I am.'

'Forget him.' He moved closer, his hand slipping to her throat, caressing her with long practised fingers as she sank back against the couch.

'He'll be worried,' she said, staring up at him.

His eyes narrowed and he stiffened. 'Is he your lover?' he asked under his breath.

'No!' His fingers bit into her throat and she gasped, but he released her immediately, sliding his fingers to the pulse that beat crazily in her throat.

'You are frightened of me,' he drawled, his smile lazy, and she shook her head.

'I'm not.'

'You mustn't be,' he said softly, and the dark shadow of his body bent over her, making her heart beat wildly. 'I don't want to hurt you,' and his hands took her waist as she sank back helplessly, seeing his face slowly come closer.

His mouth touched hers in a slow, burningly sensual kiss, making her heart thud hard as he brushed his lips to and fro against hers, teasing her with stunning expertise. The excitement took her breath away and she lay tense, immobile, her lids closed as she waited for the onslaught of the demanding kiss she knew would follow.

Mark lifted his head a fraction, his mouth next to hers as he slowly slid one hand to rest between her breasts, which were bare beneath the white silk.

'Your heart's racing,' he murmured, and she opened her lids to look at him, her eyes drugged.

'Is it?' she asked breathlessly.

His eyes never leaving her face, he lifted her hand and started to tug the fingers of her long white glove. It slithered slowly down her arm, leaving the pale flesh exposed as he put her hand to his lips and took each finger one by one into his mouth. Elizabeth caught her breath, watching with glazed eyes as he pressed his mouth to her palm, her wrist, and slowly up her naked arm to her shoulder, then to her neck.

He paused for one second, his mouth hovering

at her throat. Then his mouth fastened passionately on her throat and she gasped, clutching his head closer as he sucked the pale white flesh.

He was breathing fast now, and his mouth came to hers, fastening with an intensity that made her sink back against the couch clutching him closer to her, her hands thrusting into his hair, her bones liquid.

Mark drew back, eyes glittering, face darkly flushed. 'I must see you again,' he said deeply. 'Tomorrow night. Have dinner with me.'

Elizabeth stared. 'Yes,' she said breathlessly. What else could she say?

'I'll pick you up at eight.'

She nodded. 'I live . . .'

'I know where you live,' Mark cut in coolly, and she stared at him, again eyes wide. He studied her with cool blue eyes. 'I followed you home last night.' A smile crooked his mouth. 'At a discreet distance, of course.'

Elizabeth swallowed. 'Of course.' But her mind was flitting back to last night, desperately trying to remember the car behind her after he had given her petrol. But there wasn't a shred of evidence in her own mind that he had followed her.

Slowly she sat up, still searching her mind. Her hair was tumbling in disorganised curls around her shoulders, and she deftly began to pin it back up. Mark watched her, leaning back with a predatory gleam in his eyes as they fixed on her throat, the thin bone and muscle that strained as she clipped her hair back.

Turning, she met his intense stare and did a double-take. 'Why did you follow me all the way home?' she asked huskily. 'You must have known I'd come tonight.'

The black lashes flickered, and he hesitated. 'There was no guarantee. I knew your name and what you looked like—I didn't know your character.' He gave her a cool smile. 'For all I knew you might not have accepted the challenge, so to speak.'

Elizabeth looked at him through her lashes. 'The mind behind the face!' she said, smiling.

He whitened, and she frowned, seeing the tension in his body as he sat immobile, staring at her with stark blue eyes.

'Mark?' She leant forward, concerned.

He blinked, then gave her a tense smile. 'Sorry—I was miles away,' he said in a cool drawl. Standing up abruptly, he held out a hand to help her up. 'Shall we go? The others will wonder where we are.'

Elizabeth took his hand, standing up too and studying him with a frown. His following her for over twenty miles was very flattering—but there was something she couldn't put her finger on, something that unnerved her about his behaviour.

Mark opened the door briskly. In silence, they left the room and returned to the great hall where the party was in full swing. Eyes followed her, and Elizabeth met their stares unflinchingly. Why on earth were they staring at her like that?

She felt oddly used and a little hurt. Why the abrupt dismissal back there? After such a passionate kiss Mark had left her to walk out of the study on shaky legs, and had not spoken another word to her since.

Nicky was in the middle of a group of flushed executives as they reached him. Mark walked beside her and glanced across at Jeremy, who was being deliberately subversive, peering into a suit of armour which guarded an archway nearby. Mark's face took on a look of distaste, and Elizabeth bristled. He obviously did not like people like Jeremy.

'Hi, Liz!' Jeremy noticed her and smiled. 'Come and say hello to Rusty. He's feeling a bit empty at the moment.'

Elizabeth noted Mark Blackthorne's look of distaste, and because of that, deliberately went over to him, taking pleasure out of annoying him, although she didn't understand why. It was childish, but she couldn't help herself.

'Hello, Rusty,' she said as she joined Jeremy. He lifted up the metal visor for her to peer down, and she leant towards it, calling, 'Hello in there!' while Jeremy laughed delightedly beside her.

Nicky came over in a flash. He took Elizabeth's arm and steered her back to the main party. 'What the hell are you playing at?' he whispered anxiously in her ear. 'I'm working like crazy to drum up sponsorship and all you can do is act the fool!'

'Me?' Elizabeth gave him an innocent look.

'I expect it from Jeremy, he's half-witted as it is,' Nicky continued irritably, 'but I thought you had more sense.'

She sighed as they joined the others. Mark Blackthorne looked at her and she almost flinched from the vicious look in his eyes. But that biting anger was gone from his eyes before she could take it in, and she just stared at him open-mouthed as he shuttered his face with a smooth air, saying lazily,

'Miss Wyatt has an original sense of humour.'

Everyone laughed, but Elizabeth felt the hairs

on the back of her neck stand on end as she saw the veiled malice in Mark Blackthorne's eyes. And she was thrown totally off balance.

He had kissed her with demanding passion, as though totally obsessed with her—and now he watched her with cold cat-like malice. It made her feel uneasy, afraid. What does he want from me? she thought, staring at him.

Mayfield was still awake when they arrived home, even though it was past one o'clock in the morning. Elizabeth went into the house quietly, irritated by Nicky, who whistled triumphantly and followed her into the front room where Melanie and two of her friends were waiting up for them.

Some of the musicians who came to Mayfield lived close to the village—or close enough to be able to drive home at night and return in the morning to do some work. But the two who remained behind tonight lived on the other side of London, and had to stay at the house along with Elizabeth. Jeremy and Nicky would drive home in an hour or so, no doubt.

Elizabeth sat down while Melanie looked at Nicky with a big smile. 'How did it go?' she asked, putting her coffee cup down.

'Fantastic!' Nicky looked irritatingly superior as he stood in the middle of the room, observing Melanie down his arrogant nose. 'Although I could have asked for better behaviour from these two,' he scowled at Elizabeth and Jeremy.

Jeremy yawned. 'You're really boring, did you know that?'

'I find that infinitely preferable to being half-witted,' drawled Nicky.

'Oh?' Jeremy grinned. 'When did you make the transition?'

Nicky glared at him.

Elizabeth ignored them, feeling cold and uncomfortable in the expensive white evening dress. She wished she was wearing jeans and a sweater, and could curl up in front of the gas-fire. She unclipped her earrings and put them in her handbag, remembering suddenly how apprehensive she had been when she stood in front of the mirror hours ago and clipped them on. She had wondered then whether they made any difference to her appearance, and had sprayed on Joy perfume liberally, hoping to make an impression on Mark Blackthorne. How had she wanted him to see her? As a lady, definitely. As a cool, untouchable lady who was very much in control. And she had stumbled out of that Victorian study tonight on shaky legs, her face flushed, and her confidence falling to pieces in her hands.

She made a face to herself, as she pulled the gold necklace from her throat. That hadn't made any difference either. She caught a faint scent of Joy as she put the necklace away in her handbag and kicked off her white stilettos. Mark Blackthorne may very well have seen her as a lady, but he certainly did not think she was in control—he had seen to that with just one kiss. She flushed, remembering the way his mouth had moved hotly over her own, and unconsciously reached up one hand to touch her soft lips, as if to feel them as he had done.

Tomorrow night he would be here at eight, and she would be waiting for him. She would go through the whole rigmarole again. The cool façade would be presented with poise and elegance, only to have him smash it down with a kiss, a touch.

'Elizabeth encouraged him, of course,' Nicky was saying, and she looked up with a start, her face guilty.

'What do you mean?' she asked, feeling faint heat sting her cheeks. Was he talking about Mark Blackthorne? Did he know that he had kissed her when they were alone?

'Why?' Nicky looked at her with narrowed eyes. 'What do you think I mean?'

Elizabeth looked at the interested faces around the room. She thought quickly. Jeremy was grinning at her, blue eyes dancing. 'Jeremy!' she said as firmly as she could, and they all laughed.

All except Nicky. 'What have you been up to?' he asked slowly.

'Nothing.' She tried to look innocent.

Melanie burst out laughing 'I know that look of old!' she said, beginning to mimic their mother's voice. ' "Did you take the last chocolate biscuit, Elizabeth?" "Oh, no, Mummy, it must have been Melanie".' She shook her head, amused. 'She's lying all right.'

Nicky frowned. 'How can you tell?' he asked with a crooked smile.

'She looks too innocent.' Melanie's voice was brisk. 'She always looks innocent when she's guilty.'

There was a short pause in the conversation, and the little blonde girl who was sitting on the floor looked up. She looked like a stick-insect, but was in fact a guitarist.

'I went to the forest today,' she said dreamily, and looked at them all.

'Really?' Nicky pretended interest. The stick-insect girl rarely spoke, and when she did, no one knew quite what to say.

'Yes,' she replied, eyes shining, 'I sat in the middle of a field and smelled the grass.'

Everyone exchanged glances.

The pallid blonde girl continued, undaunted, 'It was so real, you know?' She held a guitar across her lap, plunking away at it in the same way that some people obsessively bit their fingernails. 'I thought, "I was dead and now I'm alive," you know?' Then she put the guitar down and stood up, going to the door, her jeans baggy around her thin body. 'I must get some sesame seeds and alfalfa sprouts.'

Melanie sighed as the girl closed the door behind her. 'Thank God she's going tomorrow— I don't think I could stand another lecture on junk food!'

Nicky grinned, but he looked back at Elizabeth. 'Come on, then. What is going on with you and Blackthorne?'

Elizabeth's mouth compressed. 'You're worse than a truffle hound, aren't you?' she said irritably, and he nodded grinning. She sighed. 'Mark Blackthorne is taking me out to dinner tomorrow night.'

Nicky's jaw dropped with an almost audible clang. 'You're kidding?'

Elizabeth shook her head.

'And you're going to go? Alone?'

She nodded.

Nicky pursed his lips. 'Normally I'd say it was a good idea, go right ahead.' He watched her, his face now serious. 'But I saw the way he was looking at you tonight.'

Her pulses leapt suddenly. 'How?' she asked huskily, and flushed under Nicky's penetrating gaze.

'Never you mind!' he drawled. 'Just be careful, that's all. Come back in one piece.'

Elizabeth swallowed, her mouth dry with excitement about seeing Mark again. Knowing that his interest in her had been obvious even to Nicky made her heart beat a little too fast for comfort. Mark was beginning to have a strange effect on her, and she knew that tomorrow would not come quickly enough for her.

CHAPTER THREE

HE arrived dead on the stroke of eight. Elizabeth was in her bedroom and heard him being shown into the living room by Jeremy. An ominous silence descended. Elizabeth bit her lip, hurriedly clipping her hair up high on her head. Mark wouldn't like her friends—they just weren't from his world.

Neither am I, she realised, staring at her reflection. A polished sophisticated young woman stared back, but it wasn't her. That wasn't how she felt inside. She identified more with the casual girl in jeans and no make-up who normally smiled back from her mirror. Another Elizabeth? she thought, frowning. Possibly, but her life was not built on artifice or polish. It was built on work—creative work. And if ever any artifice crept into creative work it killed it stone dead.

In a dark brown ribbed woollen dress with plunging backline and elegant collar, she was sure Mark Blackthorne would appreciate her taste in clothes. And she wanted him to appreciate her, she wanted that very much.

He was standing in the hallway when she arrived. With an air of menace he opened the front door for her and handed her her coat without a word. Elizabeth followed him outside, feeling the cold air chill her skin as she walked to the car.

He was driving a black low-slung Ferrari tonight, and he opened the door for her, going around to the other door and getting in. He was totally silent. It made Elizabeth's nerves stretch with tension as she fumbled with her seatbelt under his watchful cold gaze.

What on earth is wrong? she thought, looking at him through her lashes as he started the car with a roar and they pulled away. His face was coldly immobile, and she didn't dare to speak.

'How can you live like that?' he asked suddenly, harshly, and she stared at him in surprise.

'Like what?'

He shot her a cold look. 'You think it's perfectly normal?' he asked icily, and she blinked, her muscles tightening.

She looked away from him, watching the dark road in front of them. 'What's your definition of normal, Mr Blackthorne?' she asked quietly, and he laughed harshly under his breath.

'Don't play word games with me, Elizabeth,' he drawled coldly. 'There were at least eight people in that room, most of them filthy louts who probably spend most of their lives taking drugs of one sort or another—'

'How dare you!' she burst out angrily. 'Who the hell are you to judge them? Not one of them takes drugs; they don't even drink more than the odd glass of wine!'

'Really?' His upper lip curled in a sneer. 'You expect me to believe they're really honest, clean-cut kids, do you?'

'They may not be clean-cut,' snapped Elizabeth in an angry undertone, 'But they don't steal, they don't lie, and they don't think senseless violence is funny. That makes them just as good as the clean-cut people I've met before.'

He swung the Ferrari along the darkened road

with an angry face. 'Do they all live there?' He
shot her an icy look. 'With you?'

She flushed, her cheeks scarlet. 'No.' Looking
away from him, she said quietly, 'I lied to you
before. I don't live here, I live in London. On my
own.'

His brows shot up at that, but he didn't say
anything, just carried on driving, his strong
hands resting on the steering wheel. Elizabeth
looked at them and felt her mouth go dry as she
had a sudden memory of those long fingers
sliding around her throat. She dismissed it
immediately.

'I'm here on a working weekend,' she told him
quietly. 'The only person who lives at Mayfield is
my sister, Melanie. The others came down to
help us put together some demo tapes.'

'I see.' He indicated left as they drove through
a brightly lit town, and slowed down to park in
front of a tiny Elizabethan-fronted restaurant.
'And when do you return to London?'

'Tomorrow.' She watched him switch the
engine off, and felt suddenly too aware of him in
the plush interior of the car, which was now
silent. 'Tomorrow night.'

'And the others?'

'They all go back to their own homes
tomorrow as well. My sister will be the only one
at Mayfield until next weekend.'

'When they all descend again,' he continued for
her, a slight sneer on his upper lip. 'So it's a sort
of weekend refuge for drunken layabouts,' he
drawled sardonically. 'Is that it?'

Her eyes flashed. 'Do you take everything on
surface appearance?' she asked angrily, and
noticed him stiffen, staring at her. He was silent

for a few seconds, so she continued, 'They're professional musicians. They work incredibly hard for very little money, and sometimes have to put in eighteen hours a day.' She studied him anxiously. 'That's hardly a layabout's routine.'

He watched her. 'They just want to wriggle out of a proper job.'

'Don't be so unfair!' she exclaimed. 'They do it because they have to. They live for music—it's a labour of love.'

He turned in his seat, studying her coolly. 'I surrender,' he drawled lazily, and held up both hands. 'You've convinced me.'

Elizabeth smiled, relieved. She belonged more to the world of Mayfield than she did to Mark Blackthorne's world; he had to see that. Obviously he did—or she hoped he did.

He opened the car door and came round to help her out of the low-slung car. They walked quietly to the little restaurant, which was lit up by a yellow coach light, a creaking metal sign hanging over its door. Called the Coach House, it was a very pretty attempt to recreate the atmosphere of an Elizabethan coaching inn.

Inside, plush red carpeting and intimate lighting blended with the sturdy oak beams on ceiling and walls. A fat black cat raised its head sleepily from its position by the fireside, and regarded Elizabeth with round green eyes that looked distinctly obstinate. Totally indifferent, it lapped its front paws and plomped its head back on them as Elizabeth and Mark passed by.

Elizabeth ordered lobster and salad, while Mark had steak. As she bit into the smooth white flesh Mark watched her with a smile, and told her about an incident at Cap d'Antibes when he had ordered fresh lobster the previous year. The chef had brought the live, wriggling lobster to the table and lifted it, snapping ferociously, out of its dish, whereupon it had clipped the unfortunate chef's thumb with one hefty pincer. The chef had dropped it with a yelp, and was forced to bring another lobster to the table in its place. But this time he did not lift it out of its dish!

Over coffee, Mark stopped talking, and sat watching her with a frown. Suddenly he asked, 'Why do you want to be a singer? What is it that attracts you to that sort of life?'

Elizabeth sighed, looking up with a smile. 'I don't know. It's just something I always wanted to do.'

'But to live like that . . .' he frowned. 'You can't find it very pleasant, surely?'

She laughed, her eyes sparkling. 'You mean you wouldn't!'

He shrugged. 'Granted. But even so, it's hardly what one would call a stable lifestyle.'

Elizabeth sobered, studying him seriously. 'The lifestyle has nothing to do with it. It's the work I'm interested in. But it's more than that. It's something I have to do, or I'd regret it for the rest of my life.'

'Chasing moonbeams?' he drawled sardonically.

'We all dream,' she pointed out quietly. 'Few of us have the chance to try to make it reality.'

Mark studied her through hooded lids. 'You can't build your life on dreams.'

'I'm not trying to!' She leant forward. 'It won't make any difference if I fail publicly. Don't you see that? I don't sing for you, or Nicky, or anybody else. I sing for myself.' She held his stare and said quietly, 'I sing—full stop.'

Mark's lips crooked into a sardonic smile. 'I sing, therefore I am?' he drawled. 'Is that it?'

She nodded slowly. 'That's about as close as you can get, yes.'

He sipped his coffee, considering this, while Elizabeth eyed him with resignation. People rarely understood either her or her friends. Unless, of course, they became suddenly successful—in which case they were treated with awe and respect. She remembered the brief three months in which Gordon Eyer had risen to fame. In February he had been a scruffy musician scraping a living at little clubs, treated with contempt and despair by his family and people in authority. By July he was riding high, with a record in the Top Twenty, dressed in silk suits and treated like a returning conqueror by the very same people who had laughed at him previously.

Mark looked up suddenly, and now his eyes were intense, fixed. 'I take it marriage plays no part in your plans?'

She was taken aback. 'Well,' she shrugged, 'obviously I think about it from time to time. I'm just waiting for the right man.'

'And when you find him—' Mark said softly, 'what then?'

Elizabeth felt suddenly uneasy. 'Why do you want to know?' she asked under her breath.

His lashes flickered against the hard tanned cheekbones. 'Just curious,' he drawled smokily. 'Let's say you meet him . . . this man you would marry. Would you give it up? Your career?' The cool blue eyes were fixed on hers. 'Your lifestyle? Or would you only consider marrying a musician? Someone who could share it with you?'

Elizabeth sat very still. 'You're more than curious, Mark,' she said huskily.

He watched her carefully for a few seconds, then straightened his fingers and turned to signal for the bill. They left the restaurant a few minutes later in total silence. Elizabeth was thoughtful, excited; and was irritated with herself for feeling that way. It was absurd! She hardly knew him—of course he hadn't been thinking of marrying her! It had just been one of those occasions when fanciful dreams flitted through her head.

'It's early,' said Mark as they drove back through darkened lanes. 'Would you like to come back to Carthax for a drink?' He noticed her hesitation with a cool glance at her. 'You'll forgive me,' he said drily, 'if I don't want to spend any time at Mayfield.'

She smiled, looking at him through her lashes. 'Thank you,' she said huskily, 'I'd like that very much.'

They drove to the Carthax estate very quickly, and he led her in through the double oak doors, the blue-white light shining eerily in the cold, frosty darkness. Along the now empty corridors their footsteps echoed as he led her to the intimate Victorian study she had been in the previous night.

'I'll ask Mrs Bayliss to bring us some coffee,' he said coolly, watching her as she walked towards the fireplace, and stood tensely waiting.

When he left the room, she went over to look into the mirror which hung over the fireplace. Slowly she put her hair back into some semblance of order after the November winds had blown it loose.

Suddenly Mark was behind her. She jumped, staring at his reflection as he stood at her shoulder. The blue eyes watched her neck in a way that sent shivers of fear and excitement through her.

'Let me do that,' he said softly, and the long fingers went to her hair, slowly pinning it back up.

Elizabeth stood frozen. She stared at the dark threatening face in the mirror and realised with a sudden shock just how deeply attracted to him she was. It was magnetic, inevitable. She wished she knew why he was attracted to her, because when his eyes shone with dark cruelty she felt a premonition of fear grip her throat.

His eyes met hers in the mirror, and he smiled, exposing sharp white teeth.

'My dear,' he drawled, 'you look quite pale.'

Her eyes were enormous, deep violet, and the muscles in her neck stuck out like thin wire. She saw this in the gilt-edged mirror; saw the deep throbbing red of her mouth, and knew that she wanted him to kiss her.

'Did I tell you how lovely you look tonight?' he murmured huskily, and his head bent with hypnotic sensuality as he trailed his lips across her exposed throat.

'No,' she whispered, spellbound.

His hands slid to her shoulders, caressing her, while she shivered. Her heart thudded faster under the burning touch of his mouth on her white skin.

'You're breathtaking,' he whispered softly, and she almost moaned as his tongue snaked out across her neck.

'I enjoyed the meal,' she said breathlessly, and felt his laughter warm her skin.

'I didn't,' he drawled huskily. 'I kept thinking about this . . .' and his mouth fired hotly on her throat, making her tremble. She turned her head so that he could kiss the back of her neck while delicious shivers of pleasure rippled through her.

His hands slid around her, pulling her back against him, and she melted, her head resting limply on his shoulder as he kissed her with demanding passion, his hands holding her hips fast, pressing her tightly against him.

He raised his head a moment later, listening to her quick breathing, studying her while she simply lay back against him limply, her eyes closed in helpless submission.

She saw the quick narrowing of his eyes as he spun her, then his mouth fastened on hers in a deeply passionate kiss, his arms encircling her with a strength and power that took her breath away, making her feel tiny as she kissed him back, eyes tightly shut.

A knock on the door brought them apart, and Mark raised his head again, his skin darkly flushed. 'Yes?'

The door opened slowly, and a woman with dark hair and cold eyes came in, her face shuttered. Elizabeth felt herself flush deeply, and tried to bury her face in Mark's shoulder as he refused to let go of her.

'Coffee, sir,' the woman said in a soft, slightly unnerving voice.

'Thank you, Mrs Bayliss.' Mark dismissed her with a nod.

The woman left as quietly as she had come, and Elizabeth shuddered. She didn't like Mrs Bayliss, she decided. There was something altogether creepy about her.

Mark turned back to her, his eyes narrowed.
'Where were we?' he murmured, bending his
head, but Elizabeth put her hands at his
shoulders, saying:

'Please . . .' She flushed as he stopped,
studying her coolly. 'The coffee.' She looked over
to the leather-topped desk where Mrs Bayliss had
placed the silver tray of coffee.

The winged brows rose with amusement.
'You're not serious?' he drawled mockingly, his
eyes on her mouth.

Elizabeth looked away in confusion. 'I want
some coffee,' she said, afraid to stay in his arms
any longer. His touch sent her pulse rocketing
way out of control, and she didn't like the feeling
of not being in control. Her bones felt like liquid,
her legs were trembling, her skin was flushed.
She just couldn't think straight.

Mark watched her through dark lashes. 'You're
either very mundane or very worried. Which is
it?'

Elizabeth lowered her lashes. 'Mundane.'

'Liar,' he said softly, and caught her wrist
before she could stop him, the long fingers
touching her deftly. 'Your pulse is going like a
steam hammer.'

Elizabeth looked at him, her face serious.
'You're moving too fast for me, Mark.'

'Am I?' he murmured, and his head bent
towards her until his mouth was inches from her
own. 'Do you want me to slow down, Elizabeth?'

She stared at him, almost hypnotised by the
glittering blue eyes. 'Yes, please,' she said softly.

'Yes, please . . .' he whispered, amusement
playing on his lips, and he held her tightly for
another minute, then slowly released her, his

smile crooked. He stood back, sliding his hands into his pockets. 'Drink your coffee, then,' he drawled, and she flushed and walked over to the desk, her hands shaky as she picked up the large antique silver coffeepot. Pouring the steaming brown liquid into the two cups on the tray, she felt herself begin to calm down. Mundane? she thought with a slight smile. Perhaps. The sheer normality of the whole thing had given her back her control.

Mark was lounging against the fireplace, the polished black toes of his shoes reflecting the spitting fire. 'You must get over this fear of me, Elizabeth,' he said smokily, lids hooded. 'I intend to be with you a lot over the next few months.'

She stopped, frozen, her eyes flying open. 'How can you be so sure?' she said in a fragmented voice.

He took the cup from her deftly, putting it on the mantelpiece 'How can any of us be sure of anything?' he asked. 'We act on our instincts.'

Elizabeth watched him with wide eyes. 'And what do your instincts tell you?' she asked huskily. 'What do they tell you about me?'

Mark eyed her intently. 'Do I have to spell it out for you?' he drawled, the blue eyes darkening with sudden passion, and she flushed, her body swaying towards him.

They left a few moments later, driving back to Mayfield in silence. Elizabeth couldn't speak, she simply looked at Mark's brooding face as they drove along the dark country lanes. They pulled up outside the house, which was still brightly lit even at midnight, yellow light spilling comfortingly out of the front room window.

'I want to see you again.' Mark switched the engine off and turned to look at her coolly.

'Yes.' Her throat was tight with excitement, and he studied her with cool appraisal for a moment.

'Tomorrow night. I'll pick you up at your London flat at nine.' He took out a black leather address book, writing in bold black strokes with a silver fountain pen as Elizabeth told him her address.

He leant over, bending his black head, and his mouth claimed hers in a swift, dizzying kiss. Then drawing away as fast as he had kissed her, he held her chin in one hand, studying her with cool eyes. Elizabeth was flushed, hot, her eyes wide and confused.

'Until tomorrow,' he drawled softly, and she fumbled for the door handle and stepped out of the car.

'Goodnight,' she whispered, and he nodded as she closed the door.

Elizabeth stood on shaky legs watching the black Ferrari roar away down the street, red tail-lights flashing. Why am I so drawn to him? she asked herself.

But whatever the reason, it would make no difference. She knew that tomorrow night she would be waiting for him. And she knew that he would come.

True to his word, they saw each other constantly over the next few weeks. Elizabeth wondered how she had lived before meeting Mark—her old life seemed so empty compared with this. When she wasn't with him she was thinking of him, planning what she would wear to the new restaurant or club he would take her to.

One evening they went to his London casino,

and he gave her an enormous sum of money to play roulette with. He stood at her side, telling her which numbers to stack the black-gold chips on. When she lost he merely shrugged coolly, and when she won he shot her affectionate glances.

But as she watched him playing poker at the dimly lit table later on in the evening, she saw the cold, dispassionate face of a stranger, and her body iced with frightened tension, her world telescoping on his face. The other players were beginning to sweat as Mark edged the stakes higher, watching them all with narrowed blue eyes. Money piled up in front of his hand, breathtaking sums were being lost to him. But he remained as cold and unreadable as ever. Elizabeth suddenly realised how little she knew him; this man she was so deeply in love with, this man she felt overwhelmingly magnetised by. He was a dark, disturbing stranger.

He discovered that her favourite composer was Tchaikovsky, and got tickets for the Royal Ballet in *Swan Lake*. He had taken to buying her presents at least twice a week—sometimes a bottle of Chanel No 5 worth hundreds of pounds, sometimes a white silk blouse by Givenchy.

But tonight it was a long white silk dress. Mark Blackthorne had a penchant for Elizabeth in white—it reminded him, he said, of the night he had met her properly at his party. And as she stood in the living room of her London flat, he came up behind her to clasp a little red velvet choker around her neck.

An exquisite touch, but it made her shiver as she drove to the Opera House in the limousine with him, for around her neck the choker was as warm and sickly as freshly spilt blood.

A hush descended on the glittering array of people in the foyer of the Opera House as they walked in. Elizabeth faltered in her step, aware that all eyes were upon them, and glanced at Mark in confusion.

'Ignore them,' he murmured, bending his dark head, his black hair clean and freshly washed. He looked darkly attractive in a black evening suit, a red carnation in his lapel, a black evening cloak around his broad shoulders with a red silk lining.

But how could she ignore them? Sitting in the darkened box, she felt their stares acutely. The gilt chair she sat in straightened her back, and she glanced at Mark to see him leaning casually beside her, his eyes narrowed with cool amusement. Why did it leave him amused? Surely he should feel as uncomfortable as she did?

Towards the end of the ballet, as the Swan Queen and her Prince cast themselves into the lake, the haunting strains of the music caught her attention totally until she felt Mark's eyes burning into her. The music reached a crescendo as she turned her head to meet his gaze.

Their eyes held in an intense lock for a few seconds. Then Mark whispered intently, 'Don't ever die, Elizabeth,' and his hand caught hers in a tight hold.

Elizabeth was taken aback, and the alarm showed in her blue eyes. Mark relaxed his grip, and smiled self-deprecatingly,

'At least,' he murmured with wry amusement, 'Don't die before me!'

It was the first sign of love she had had from him, and it had made her clench with moving happiness. He did love her, after all. She hugged those words to herself for weeks, thinking of

them every time her faith in him deserted her—
and it deserted her too often for comfort.

Because something was not quite right. She
knew it, felt it deeply—something she couldn't
put her finger on, however hard she tried. From
his actions it should have been obvious that he
cared for her, but however attentive he was,
however many presents he gave her, she still felt
unsure.

Every day she felt the fear that he would not
come. There would be no phone call, no Mark.
When he went away for a few days on business—
a business he never at any time discussed with
her—she waited in agony for his calls. He sent
her red roses three times a week. Sometimes her
little flat was filled with them; and all long
stemmed blood-red roses, in silver baskets,
making the air scented, reminding her of him.

She sighed now, sitting in the living room of
her flat with a music paper open on her lap. She
had long since given up any hope of trying to
read it. That was another thing that disturbed
her.

Mark had driven out all thought of her career
since she had met him. It was two weeks now
since she had been in touch with Nicky, two
weeks since she'd been to Mayfield for the
weekend. At first she had tried to live both lives,
but it had been impossible. One had nudged out
the other, and now her only life was the one she
led with Mark.

He was coming tonight. She had begun to plan
her life around him. It seemed natural now to
spend the whole day thinking of him, waiting for
him. She was obsessed with him.

The telephone rang, jolting her, and snatching

up the receiver, she felt her heart thump wildly in the hope that it was him.

'I'll pick you up at eight.' Mark's deep voice made her whole body come alive, ripples running across her flesh as she clutched the receiver tightly. 'Sorry it's so late, but my flight was delayed, and I had to wait at Rome airport for three hours.'

Elizabeth felt a smile curve her lips. 'You poor thing! I thought it was something like that.' The relief she felt was indescribable. He had been in Italy for two days, promising to ring her this morning. But the hours had ticked past with deathly slowness, as they always did until she heard from him.

You weren't worried, then?' Mark asked dryly.

'Only a little,' she replied, smiling. Understatement of the year, she thought with a grin.

Mark laughed huskily at the other end of the line. 'You just happened to be sitting by the phone, I suppose?' he drawled, and she felt herself flush with colour,

'Don't tease me, Mark,' she said quietly, feeling a fool. She could have kicked herself for snatching up the phone on the first ring. Why didn't I let it ring for a while? she thought angrily.

Mark was silent for a moment, then he said gently, 'I'm sorry.'

'That's okay.' She twisted the cord in one slim hand. 'Where are we going tonight?'

'Dinner in my suite,' he told her coolly. 'I'd like you to wear the white dress—the one you wore to the ballet.'

'Oh?' she frowned, perplexed. Surely she would be overdressed?

Darling,' he drawled, 'have you forgotten? It's our anniversary. We met one month ago tonight.'

She caught her breath in surprise. 'Mark . . .' she began, but he broke in coolly to say:

'I'll see you at eight. I have some things to attend to now.'

The line went dead. Elizabeth felt her mouth compress. He was always doing that, especially if he rang during business hours. She wished he wasn't so abrupt.

But as she replaced the ivory receiver, she smiled. He had remembered! Wasn't it supposed to be the woman who ringed the days on her calendar, like a fool? She sighed happily and dashed into her bedroom to change into her white wrap before running her bath. Tonight was obviously going to be a special night—worthy of the Chanel No 5 body lotion he had bought her a week ago! Taking her white dress out of the wardrobe, she held it in front of her.

Suddenly she stopped short, as she caught sight of her face in the dressing table mirror. Is this love? she thought, staring. Slowly she sat down on the edge of the bed, looking long and hard into her mirror.

The eyes that watched her were her own, but for these few rare seconds they were open, clear. All the barriers we normally erect to the world leave our eyes looking merely like eyes, never windows. But now as she stared intently Elizabeth saw them change, become deep almost purple, and she felt she could look right through them, down into her soul. And in that moment she saw herself stripped bare, saw her capacity for emotion—a capacity which shook her badly, because she suddenly realised just how much

Mark could hurt her if he ever chose to. She felt too much for him. Too much.

The painful realisation made her turn her head away from her own eyes. The silence in the little bedroom was suddenly overwhelming. Pushing away her thoughts, she stood up slowly, and went into the bathroom to get ready. It was easier not to think about it; it was easier just to feel. Because at the back of her mind lay the frightening suspicion that Mark did not feel as much for her, and that was something she was simply not ready to face.

He arrived dead on time, as usual. Elizabeth went downstairs to greet him, her long white dress rippling in the December breeze as she opened the door. The red velvet choker lay around her white throat; she had known he would expect her to wear it too.

'Happy anniversary,' he drawled, and bent his head to kiss her. 'You look ravishing.'

She felt a pulse throb in her throat as his lips brushed her own. 'Thank you for remembering,' she said, closing the front door a moment later and linking her arm through his as they walked to the car.

He shot her an amused glance. 'You forgot, I suppose?'

'Of course not! I just thought you would.'

His mouth curved in a sardonic smile. 'Oh, I never forget anything,' he drawled, and she believed him only too well. There was something quintessentially ruthless about him, about those narrowed blue eyes.

She watched him open the rear door of the limousine. 'Like the elephant?' she asked with a little smile, and his winged brows rose.

'An elephant?' he said, laughing ruefully. 'That's not quite what I had in mind!'

Elizabeth laughed too, her eyes shining. 'Don't take me so literally!'

His eyes darkened. 'I'll take you any way I can,' he murmured, and his gaze burnt on her mouth for a second, making her breath catch. Then he opened the door wider, saying, 'Get in before I kiss you.' His eyes glittered, 'I wouldn't want to shock your neighbours!'

Elizabeth got into the car, feeling more relaxed. He was in a very good mood tonight, obviously because of the occasion. She suddenly wondered whether he intended making love to her tonight.

The thought made her pulses leap. He had drawn back at the last moment every time she had seen him. They spent long evenings together, constantly touching each other in surreptitious, tense ways, and would go back to his penthouse suite at the end of the evening.

There, Mark seduced her with expert hands, lying alongside her on the couch, his hands wringing frenzied excitement from her until she felt herself want to slide to her knees. But always, at the last minute, he would draw back and study her coolly—just when she expected him to swing her into his arms and kick open the door to the master bedroom.

Perhaps tonight would not end with that heated, liquid frustration. Perhaps tonight he would kick open that door. The thought made her pulses skid crazily.

'Jean-Jacques is giving us pheasant tonight,' Mark told her as they stepped out of the lift on to the top floor of the Park Lane building, 'and a bottle of Dom Perignon is chilling for us.'

Elizabeth smiled. 'Wonderful!' she said with admirable restraint, because secretly she wanted to fling her arms round him. But she didn't quite feel able to show so much affection, which was another thing that bothered her.

'I'm glad you're pleased,' he drawled, standing in the hallway and watching her with amusement.

Elizabeth reached up on tiptoe to kiss him. 'I've never had an anniversary before,' she said, looking up into his eyes. 'Have you?'

His face shuttered. She watched as the hooded lids came down, and his face turned into a cold unreadable mask. Sliding her hands from his shoulders, he turned away in silence and walked towards the door which led to the dining room.

'We'll go straight in, shall we?' he said coolly.

Elizabeth watched him, perplexed. She felt confused and a little hurt. But she smiled and walked towards the door as he pushed it open.

Her breath caught as she walked inside. 'My God . . .!' she whispered, staring.

A hundred candles flickered around the room, standing in antique silver candelabra. They gleamed in the polished oak room, and she stared incredulously, spellbound with wonder.

Mark watched with brooding eyes. 'You like it?'

Turning, she said huskily, 'It's beautiful,' and the flames leapt in her violet eyes. She was deeply moved by the romanticism of the gesture.

Mark walked towards her. 'Good.' Seating her at the table, he picked up a single white rose and handed it to her. 'It reminds me of you,' he murmured, and brushed his mouth over hers.

Elizabeth clutched the white rose, and thorns dug into her flesh. 'Oh!' She dropped the rose in dismay, as scarlet blood sprang from her fingertip.

The blue eyes narrowed disconcertingly on her hand. 'You've cut yourself, my dear,' he drawled in a voice so soft it made her heart stop. Slowly he took her hand, studying the blood on her white flesh.

Elizabeth watched, breathless, feeling the sensuality engulf her as his mouth fastened on her skin and he sucked the blood gently at her fingertip.

Their eyes met. Darkness leapt in his eyes, and he bent his head hungrily, parting her lips with sudden drowning passion while she let her lids close. Her hands came up to twine in his thick black hair, and she felt his heart thudding faster against her own, her pulses quickening.

The door opened, and Mark's head spun round, knives leaping from his eyes. Jean-Jacques came in in his white chef's cap, carrying a large silver dish before him. He watched them haughtily, ignoring Mark's vicious stare. Then placing the dish on the table, he bowed with Gallic arrogance, and left the room.

Mark released her, the moment over, and sat opposite her. His dark face lit up by a hundred flickering candleflames, he poured champagne into her glass, raising his own in a toast.

Elizabeth clinked her glass against his in the silent toast, and drank the cool champagne, feeling the bubbles sting the back of her throat.

After dinner, Mark watched her across the now empty table, the yellow dancing flames of the candles giving her a strange sensation of being transported back in time as they gleamed on the oak table and walls.

'Do you remember our first evening together?' Mark asked coolly, watching her with narrowed eyes.

Elizabeth smiled. 'Of course! The little restaurant in Essex.'

He inclined his head. 'Do you remember I asked how you felt about marriage?'

Her heart stopped. She nodded, silent.

Mark observed her through hooded lids. 'How do you feel about it now?'

She just stared, her eyes enormous, unable to speak. There was a little silence, and she tried to think of something to say, but she knew she couldn't. She was simply waiting, breathless, for him to continue.

He studied her intently. 'My dear,' he drawled, his voice dry, 'I'm asking you to marry me.'

Elizabeth just looked at him, incredulous. He took a little blue velvet box from his pocket and laid it on the table. Opening the lid, he turned it towards her. An antique silver ring glittered on the blue velvet. Diamonds circled an enormous ruby, and she caught her breath, her heart thudding too fast.

'It's yours,' he said softly, 'if you'll be mine.'

Elizabeth slowly raised her eyes to his, tears shining in them so that she saw his dark face through a mist in which flames danced and wavered. 'I've always been yours,' she said huskily.

He seemed to relax, exhaling slowly. Then he stood up, coming round to where she sat and holding her hand as he took the ring from its box.

Slowly he slid the ring on to her finger where it sparkled, blood-red against her snow-white skin, and she looked at it with inexpressible happiness.

'I love you,' she whispered, and waited for him to say it too, but he just watched her, his blue eyes cool. Elizabeth felt a shiver of alarm.

'We'll get married next month,' he told her.

CHAPTER FOUR

NICKY and Melanie screamed round to Elizabeth's London flat as soon as they heard. Mark had put an announcement in *The Times* a week after they were engaged, and Nicky had obviously read it, because he arrived at her flat in a state of incoherence.

'What about your career?' demanded Nicky as he stood in the living room, towering over her. 'You only have to take one look at Blackthorne to see he'll want you at home with him.'

'I've discussed it with him already,' Elizabeth told him firmly, 'and he said I could go ahead with it.'

Nicky eyed her with angry suspicion. 'Does he realise what's involved? The work you have to put in day by day already?'

She frowned. 'Of course! He knows I work hard on my vocal exercises already.'

Nicky snorted. 'Has he heard you sing?'

'Well,' Elizabeth bit her lip, 'not exactly . . .'

'I thought as much!' Nicky snapped angrily. 'I haven't heard from you for three weeks. Three weeks! I can just imagine how much work you've been doing! Too busy mooning over Mark Blackthorne.'

'I'm sorry,' Elizabeth said quietly. 'I was too busy seeing Mark. I kept meaning to ring you, but the longer I left it, the more scared I was.'

'Scared?' shouted Nicky, eyes black with offence. 'Of me? Since when have I ever given you cause to be scared of me?'

Elizabeth glared at him. 'I wish I had a tape recorder! If you could only hear yourself!'

He glowered at her like a thundercloud. 'What the hell does that mean?' he demanded angrily.

Melanie sighed, interceding, 'Oh, shut up, Nicky!'

He stared at her in disbelief.

Melanie eyed him calmly. 'Shouting won't help. Stop huffing and puffing like a big bad wolf—you only frighten yourself.'

Nicky sat down slowly, speechless.

Elizabeth gave Melanie a thankful smile and said, 'Look, I couldn't have concentrated on singing even if I had rung you. I know it sounds silly, but that's because you're not ... well,' she floundered, not wanting to expose the depth of her feelings to them.

Melanie smiled. 'I understand, Lizzie,' she said warmly, and looked at Nicky with irritation. 'Even if Adolf here doesn't.'

Nicky scowled. 'Very funny!'

'But you ought to have telephoned,' Melanie reproved. 'It is nearly Christmas, after all. It was very naughty of you.'

Elizabeth smiled, glancing out of the window at the brightly lit street outside. Christmas lights hung in the houses opposite, fake snow clung to the windowpanes, and a few golden Merry Christmas signs peered out between the curtains. Elizabeth's living room was decorated too, with pretty paper chains circling the walls and meeting in the centre at the light.

Mark had helped her decorate the room, and the memory made her flush, her heart quickening. He had held her waist as she stood on her little step-ladder, Sellotaping the chains to the light cord. They had both decorated the tree, which Mark had brought in for her one Sunday afternoon, and as the chill winter sunshine shone in through the window, they had hung pretty decorations on it, brightly coloured balls and stars with a stiff golden-haired fairy perched uncomfortably at the top of the tree, her arms stuck out woodenly.

'Does this mean that you won't be doing any work until after the wedding?' asked Nicky, his face sullen with bad temper.

Elizabeth sighed and went over to the window, looking at the narrow suburban street below. 'I don't know, Nicky,' she murmured, fingering the lace curtains. 'It doesn't seem likely—there'll be so much to do.'

'And I'll just have to shelve everything for you?' Nicky was working himself up into another fury, and Melanie stood up quickly.

'Stop it, Nicky,' she said briskly. 'I won't have you spoiling her wedding. You'll just have to wait.'

'For how long?' he snapped. 'I had everything set up. R.C.I. were willing to hear the demo tapes next month, and now it won't be till February. How long do you think they'll wait?'

Elizabeth bit her lip. 'Look, it's just until the honeymoon is over.' She gave him a pleading smile, her eyes anxious.

He considered her for a moment, then huffed, sitting back in his seat with a sigh. 'Oh, very well,' he muttered. 'I suppose the Blackthorne marriage will do your image a lot of good, at least.'

She laughed. 'I might have known you'd think of that!' It hadn't even occurred to her, she had been too busy trying to figure out if Mark really loved her. But Nicky had thought of it. Nicky always did. That was why he was such a good manager, after all. Even if he did shout and bellow appallingly—if he wasn't such a strong character, he wouldn't be able to handle record companies so well.

Melanie went over to the little record player that sat on the floor in the corner of the room, and selected a current Top Ten hit album, putting it on the turntable. A minute later the loud strains of the first hit from the album floated through the room.

'I vote,' said Melanie, 'that we have a drink to celebrate Lizzie's engagement.'

Nicky rubbed a weary hand over his eyes. 'I'll never understand women if I live to be a hundred!'

'Which isn't likely, from the way you're behaving at the moment,' retorted Melanie, and he made a face at her. She laughed and went into the kitchen to get Elizabeth's only bottle of wine from the fridge.

Elizabeth followed her into the narrow kitchen, leaning against the wall as she got glasses from the cupboard over the fridge.

Melanie stopped unscrewing the cork from the wine as she saw Elizabeth watching her. 'What's wrong?' she asked quietly.

Elizabeth shrugged, looking down at her hands. 'I just wanted to apologise,' she gave a little smile, 'for being such a pest!'

Melanie laughed, pulling the corkscrew up so that the cork came up with a loud popping sound. 'I hate sisters who apologise!' she said, embarrassed, and Elizabeth laughed too. Melanie peered into the corridor to see if Nicky was listening, then said quickly, 'Can I see your ring again?'

Elizabeth held out her hand, and the ruby flashed under the white glare of the kitchen light.

'God, it's enormous!' Melanie breathed, holding Elizabeth's finger. 'It must have cost an absolute fortune.' She frowned. 'Aren't rubies supposed to be unlucky?'

Elizabeth tilted her head to one side, murmuring, 'Not that I know of,' and took her hand away, looking down at the clear blood-red stone with a frown.

Melanie watched her for a moment, then turned and started filling the glasses with wine. 'You know how much I hate being soppy,' she said in a quiet voice, 'but I hope you'll be very happy, and it all works out for you both . . . and all the rest of that stuff!' She grinned, looking over her shoulder, her cheeks pink with embarrassment. 'Well, you know.'

Elizabeth grinned back. 'I do indeed!' she said, and Melanie chuckled, picking up the glasses and carrying them into the living room where Nicky sat sulking in a chair.

Elizabeth hoped rubies weren't unlucky. Mark had been as attentive as ever. His actions told her clearly that he loved her. But still she wasn't sure of him. Still she fretted anxiously when he wasn't with her. They had sent out the gilt-edged invitations a couple of days ago, and she had felt a thrill of pride as she saw her name coupled with his. Soon she would be Elizabeth Blackthorne, and she sometimes found herself doodling the name on pieces of odd paper, a ridiculous smile curving her lips. But it wasn't as it should be. And the knowledge that there was something wrong had been making her upset and worried all week.

*   *   *

They drove down to Carthax House on Christmas Eve. Mark wanted her to spend Christmas with him, and she had been in an agony of excitement for the week preceding Christmas. They sat in the back of the limousine now as they drove to Essex in the late afternoon.

'You'll like Abigail,' Mark was saying as they sped past wind-blown meadows in the car. 'She's a real individual—always has been.'

'How old is she?' asked Elizabeth, trying to picture his sister. His parents had both died ten years ago, and he had only one living close relative—just as she had. It was one of those strange coincidences, and the fact that they both had only one sister living made her feel closer to him, as though she could understand him better because of his past.

Mark laughed. 'She'd never forgive me if I told you!' he drawled, a smile playing on his lips. 'She looks a lot younger than she is. Someone once called her "well preserved", and she blew into a temper. But she's younger than me, if that's what you're asking.'

Elizabeth smiled. 'I was just trying to imagine her, that's all.'

He shot a sidelong look at her. 'Forget it,' he drawled. 'It's impossible. She's an artist—in her spare time now. Although she once had hopes of being a female Salvador Dali.'

'Really?' her brows rose. 'Is she any good?'

'Oh yes,' said Mark, lighting a cigarette, silver-blue smoke curling from its glowing tip. 'Her work is startlingly vivid. Dark, mysterious paintings straight from the unconscious. A mixture of Rousseau and Dali—surrealist and very primitive.' He gave her an amused look, his blue eyes glittering. 'Plenty of Jungian imagery.'

'But not Freudian?' said Elizabeth, cheeks dimpling, and he laughed, looking at her through sooty lashes.

'You,' he drawled, 'have a wicked mind.'

Elizabeth gave him a shy smile as the car swung into the grounds of his estate. Only one car stood on the gravel driveway, and Mark looked at it with a cool expression.

'They're here already,' he drawled, and Elizabeth looked at him, catching the cold undertone of his voice. She was used to all its nuances now, and it had so many. But she could detect instantly when his mood was changing—she just couldn't see what he was thinking. That, she thought as they stepped out of the car, is what I'll have to work on next.

They went into the house, walking along the echoing corridors and into a main living room which Elizabeth had never seen before. Cream and gold walls were hung with wide gilt-edged mirrors. Pale green brocade furniture stood on a cream carpet, while huge green plants sat in ivory and gold pots around the room.

A sloe-eyed woman with black hair stood by the fireplace in a black silk dress, looking like a Russian countess as she held a glass of brandy to her red mouth.

She looked up as Elizabeth came in—and gasped, the black eyes widening. The glass slipped from her fingers, shattering on the hearth, brandy seeping into the cream rug she stood on.

Elizabeth looked at Mark, alarmed, but he just closed the door behind them with a cool click.

'Abigail,' he drawled, 'no melodramatics, please.'

Abigail looked at Elizabeth with wide eyes, then shook her head, looking down at the shattered glass. 'Oh,' she said, and her voice trembled a little, 'I'm sorry.' She gave a little smile which did not reach her startled eyes. 'You made me jump.'

Mark walked into the room, sliding his hands into his pockets. 'You frightened Elizabeth,' he said coolly, and his sister clasped her hands in front of her, sighing,

'I'm so sorry.' She came across the room to Elizabeth, who was feeling distinctly uneasy, and shook her hand. 'I've been looking forward to meeting you.'

Elizabeth gave her a ghost of a smile. 'Thank you.'

Abigail slid her hands into the pockets of her silk dress. 'Come and sit down by the fire, you must be so cold.' She walked Elizabeth over to the pale green brocade couch. 'I'll get you a drink. What'll it be? Gin? Whisky?'

'Stop fussing,' drawled Mark, and his sister threw him an angry look.

'I'm only trying to make her feel at home,' she said with a snap. 'I thought that's what you'd want.'

Elizabeth jumped at the biting anger in Abigail's voice, and looked at Mark, bewildered, hoping to find an explanation in his eyes. But they were cool, and narrowed on his sister's flushed face.

'Where's Jim?' Mark asked coldly, and his sister jerked her head towards the door.

'Upstairs,' she replied with a snap, 'unpacking.'

Mark eyed her. 'Call him down.'

Abigail's lips compressed. 'Stop talking about him as if he was a dog!' she said irritably, and turned back to Elizabeth. Seeing the look of bewildered unease on her face, she smiled gently. 'Don't pay any attention to us,' she said with a warm smile. 'We always argue like this.'

'Oh?' Elizabeth did not quite believe that.

Abigail's face broke into a wide smile, her eyes almost sloping into her ears, lined with black colour. 'I'm afraid so!' she said, laughing. 'You'll have to get used to it. We never could stand the sight of each other, could we, brother dear?'

Mark seemed to relax, leaning against the wall. 'Never,' he agreed, cool amusement in his eyes.

'He used to try to knock my front teeth out,' said Abigail with a bright smile which didn't quite reach her eyes, 'Now he just bores them out.'

Mark pushed away from the wall and went over to the drinks cabinet. 'You're asking for trouble, Abigail,' he said smoothly.

Abigail laughed, giving him a sidelong glance. 'I'd like to see you try anything,' she said, 'with Khan around.'

'Khan?' queried Elizabeth, in hopeless confusion, trying to change the subject because the barbed remarks were disturbing.

'Kubla Khan—my dog,' Abigail told her. 'Mark thinks he's a horse, but that's just because he's scared stiff of him, aren't you, Mark?'

Mark shot his sister a wry look over his shoulder. 'Don't be ridiculous, Abigail,' he told her coolly. Then he turned, bringing a glass of sherry over to Elizabeth and saying, 'He's an enormous Dobermann. He even worries my Alsatians, and there are eight of them.'

Elizabeth's eyes widened. 'Eight? That's almost a pack!'

He laughed. 'They guard the estate,' he told her wryly. 'They each have a separate handler. Don't worry, darling, they won't attack you.'

Footsteps approached outside, then the door opened and a man of about thirty came in. He was beginning to lose his hair, and the tawny mass was swept back, showing a long widow's peak with pale skin climbing on either side. He wore a casual outfit of baggy country trousers and a vee-neck sweater with a diamond pattern. 'Hello, all,' he said lazily, and behind him padded the biggest, blackest dog Elizabeth had ever seen.

'Good God!' she breathed, staring at it. It was so big that it was at waist height to the man who came in, and its silky coat rippled with strong muscles, its noble face immediately homing in on Elizabeth as he scented a stranger.

'My husband, Jim Carter,' said Abigail, and pointed to Elizabeth. 'This is the fiancée— Elizabeth,' she said in a dry voice, and Jim Carter did a visible double-take, his mouth hanging open in surprise.

'My God!' he said stupidly, staring at her with wide tawny eyes, then he shook his head and came forward, as did the dog. 'Sorry! Just a little surprised to see you here so soon.'

But as he shook hands with her, Elizabeth saw him exchange baffled looks with his wife, who just shrugged and made meaningful faces at Mark.

Elizabeth shifted uneasily in her chair. She tried to catch Mark's eye, but he was deliberately avoiding looking at her. Why did they both stare at her so much? she thought, desperately worried.

She remembered the party she had attended here all those weeks ago. She remembered the way the guests had stared at her as she walked past, and a frown of deep worry etched itself into her brow. She bit her lip as she looked at Mark, wondering what on earth was going on.

Mark noticed her expression and his eyes narrowed. 'I'll show you your room,' he said quickly, pushing away from the fireplace where he had been lounging casually. 'Dinner is at seven,' he told the other two. 'I'll see you down here then. And don't be late, Mrs Bayliss always times everything to the last minute.'

Abigail made a face. 'And we wouldn't want to upset Mrs Bayliss, would we?'

Jim laughed, his face creasing up in a rueful expression. 'Heavens, no!' he exclaimed, hands in his baggy trousers, grinning at his wife. 'She's a real harridan, isn't she? Can't think why you keep her, Mark.'

'She does her job.' Mark gave him a dry look and led Elizabeth out into the corridor, closing the door behind them.

They walked up the main staircase in silence, and Elizabeth was grateful when he took her hand in his at the top of the long staircase, because her thoughts were whizzing frantically. Abigail had reacted in a bizarre way—*très bizarre*, she thought to herself, frowning as the memory flickered back vividly. It would have been easy to dismiss if Jim hadn't been just as shocked to see her sitting there. It was another in a long line of things about Mark that just did not add up.

'I thought I'd put you in here,' said Mark, pushing open a thick oak door.

Elizabeth walked into the bedroom with an

incredulous expression. A huge fourposter bed dominated the room. Long red velvet curtains hung around it, the posts decorated with exquisite carvings. The walls were oak-panelled, the windows criss-crossed with lead. Huge French windows opened on to the balcony.

She turned to look at Mark. 'What an incredible room!' she said, laughing under her breath. 'I feel like a princess!'

Mark closed the door, sliding his hands into his pockets. 'Yes, it is nice, isn't it?' he drawled, glancing around the room. 'Straight out of a storybook.'

Elizabeth walked over to the bed. 'I used to dream about a bed like this when I was a little girl.' Running her fingers along the carved wooden posts, she looked over her shoulder at him. 'My mother used to tell me bedtime stories—all about princesses with long golden hair who lived in big castles. I wanted to be like them.'

Mark tilted his head to one side, his eyes tender. 'I prefer dark-haired princesses myself!'

She laughed. 'I had very corny fantasies!'

'Don't we all?' he murmured, and continued studying her in silence, making her brow crease with a frown. He noticed her expression and smiled ruefully. 'I'm sorry—I didn't mean to stare—I just can't picture you as a little girl.'

'No,' she said thoughtfully, 'no, I don't suppose you can.' Folding her arms, she studied him with an affectionate smile. 'I was, though, I'm afraid. Very little. And very naughty, too!'

He laughed, coming across to where she stood. 'Now that I can picture!' he slid his arms round her waist, looking down at her. Lights danced in his eyes. 'Did you run amok?'

Her cheeks dimpled. 'What's a mok?'

He laughed, bending his head until his lips brushed hers in a gentle kiss. His arms drew her closer, one hand going to support the back of her head as she wound her own arms slowly around his neck.

She bent her head after he had kissed her, nestling her face in his shoulder. She could smell the clean fresh scent of his black hair, feel the warmth of his body at the throat.

'Mark,' she said quietly, 'why did your sister drop her glass like that?' Drawing back, she looked up at him. 'When I first arrived?'

He looked suddenly cagey. 'I really don't know,' he drawled, his mouth turning down at the corners as he shrugged. 'Maybe she was just startled.'

She frowned, considering this. 'No, I think it was more than that. She was staring at me in a very odd way. Didn't you notice?'

He grew remote. 'Not at all. Abigail is an artist—in every sense of the word. She has a flair for melodrama. When we were kids she used to scare my mother out of her wits by screaming the house down over some tiny graze.' He smiled. 'My mother always thought it was something serious and came running in a panic.' He laughed, and his eyes glittered. 'Abigail used to get smacked a lot for it.'

Elizabeth smiled too, but refused to give up. 'Jim did it too, though,' she said as casually as possible. 'He looked just as shocked when he saw me.'

Mark sighed, releasing her slowly. A frown pulled his black brows together. 'I think you're just being over-sensitive, darling.'

She caught his arm. 'I disagree,' she said in a low voice. 'People have been staring like that ever since I met you. At the ballet, at the theatre— even at your party. You may not have noticed it, but I certainly have.'

He studied her coldly. 'It's your imagination.' He turned with an abruptness that upset her, and walked towards the door. 'I'll send your case up. Dinner will be an hour or so. You have plenty of time to change.'

He closed the door on her, and she sighed heavily and sank down on to the bed, fingering the heavy red velvet curtains with a distracted frown.

Why did he turn away from her when it was important that she understand? It just wasn't normal for his sister to react like that—dropping her glass and gasping! That wasn't the way a woman greeted her brother's future wife. What was it that had made Abigail so shocked? Elizabeth frowned, then got up slowly and walked over to the dressing table.

She sat down, and her eyes sought the looking-glass. Only her own face stared back at her. She reached up one hand slowly, and traced the outline of her high cheekbones. The white, white skin and ruby red lips were nothing to be afraid of. The enormous black-fringed violet eyes were nothing that could shock. So why had Abigail stared at her like that?

As if she was a ghost ... Elizabeth sighed, leaning on the dressing table. It was inexplicable. Just as so many things about Mark were inexplicable.

Close to seven o'clock, she went down the wide sweeping staircase, her feet soft on the heavy red carpet which was pinned to the wooden steps by gold bars. She wore a white silk suit, the skirt narrow, outlining her slender shape. The jacket was soft silk, with padded shoulders. Beneath it she wore a black silk shirt and a gold necklace, which gleamed at her throat like a coiled snake.

Biting her lip, she looked up and down the long corridors which led off each side of the wide hall. Which way had they come? Which way was the drawing room? Frowning, she tried to get her bearings.

The chandelier tinkled softly as the wind outside pushed in through a small window open in the hall. The crystal teardrops brushed against each other softly, gilt against glass, the light glowing brightly.

Suddenly she heard voices. They came from the right-hand corridor. Elizabeth turned and began walking towards the voices, her feet muffled by the plush red deep-pile carpet of the corridor. Was that Mark's voice she heard, raised for a few seconds, then lowering with sudden quiet intensity? She frowned, trying to see which room they came from.

Then the voices stopped, and her footsteps halted. Walking to the nearest oak door, she reached for the handle, about to look inside to see if they were in there, but just as her fingers touched the polished brass doorknob the voices started up again from inside.

'You must be mad!' Abigail's voice came low and angry behind the oak door, and Elizabeth froze, unable to stop listening, but unable to move away.

'I quite agree,' drawled Mark, his voice closer to the door than his sister's, and Elizabeth frowned, wondering what they were talking about. 'I must be—to stand here and listen to this!'

'It isn't funny,' Abigail muttered, and her footsteps rang out as she began to pace the room, heels clicking on the polished wood floor. 'I know damned well what you're up to. It's always the same, isn't it? Another girl, another face—I can read your mind like a book!'

There was a slight pause, then Mark drawled coldly, 'Mind your own business, Abigail.'

'It is my business. I'm your sister, for God's sake!' Abigail's voice was lowered, intense, and Elizabeth had to lean closer to the door to hear her words. 'And I won't stand by and watch you do this!'

Glass hit glass as Mark poured himself a drink. 'Just stay out of it,' he muttered.

A chandelier shook inside the room and Elizabeth heard Abigail say, 'Not this time, Mark.' There was a tense silence, then she continued, 'It's too risky. What if she goes to the West Wing? We all know what she'll find there, don't we? What if she stumbles on to it?'

'I'll tell her soon, myself,' Mark said in an undertone.

'Like hell you will!' Abigail muttered angrily. 'You'll just lock up the West Wing and try to pretend it doesn't exist.' She paused for a moment and then Elizabeth heard her say, almost to herself, 'Maybe I should take her there myself.'

Elizabeth heard Mark put his glass down on the table with tight control. 'I'm warning you,' he said tensely, 'don't meddle in my affairs.'

Abigail ignored the warning. 'She's only a child,' she said in a low voice, and began pacing the room again. 'How old is she? Twenty? Twenty-one?' A silence, then, 'I thought so. My God, you're sick!'

Mark gave an icy laugh that chilled Elizabeth's blood. 'Has it ever occurred to you that I might love her?'

'Never in a million years, you bastard!'

'Do you really believe I'd marry a woman I didn't care for?' he snarled.

'You're capable of anything! That's why you're going through with this farce! Just like all the others. Only this time you're going to marry her. And you'll kill her, just like you killed——'

'I'm warning you!' he bit out. 'Stay out of it!'

Elizabeth stumbled away from the door in shock, her eyes wide but blinded. Her body was too clumsy, and she stumbled into a small table, knocking it over, and an antique silver music box went flying from the top of the mahogany table.

Elizabeth gasped. In slow motion she watched, horrified. The little silver music box flew as though floating, towards the floor with the table tipping over as it fell.

The table thudded heavily on the floor with a sickly thud. The silver music box crashed on to the polished wood, and the lid flew open. Ghostly strains of haunting music began to tinkle from the open lid, making the silence in the other room suddenly frighteningly noticeable.

'Someone's outside!' Abigail's harsh whisper made her react instantly.

Adrenalin flooded her body as she pushed open a door opposite and dived into the darkened room. Hiding behind the door, she held her breath, shivering from the icy breeze from an open window.

Mark's footsteps raced to the door, yanking it open, sending it crashing back on its hinges. Abigail's footsteps were right behind her brother's as Elizabeth sensed them both standing in the doorway beside the upturned table and music box.

'Who's there?' Mark demanded bitingly.

The little silver music box played its ghostly music as if in reply. Elizabeth held her breath, her heart pounding dangerously. Eyes closed, she prayed they wouldn't discover her. She pressed tightly against the wall, hearing her own heart thud in a loud giveaway rhythm.

'The library!' said Abigail, breathing hard. 'The door's open.'

Mark's footsteps came towards the room Elizabeth hid in. She heard him breathing as he stood in the darkened doorway, and the seconds stretched eternally as she held her breath.

Suddenly the light flicked on, flooding the room with light. 'Who's there?' asked Mark in a low, dangerous voice.

The only reply was the howling gale outside. Rain beat against the open window, spattering on to a pile of books which lay on the windowsill. Elizabeth prayed that he wouldn't look behind the door.

She heard him breathe out slowly. 'There's no one in here,' he muttered, and Abigail joined him in the doorway.

'Maybe the wind blew the table over,' she suggested.

He gave a harsh crack of laughter. 'Don't be crazy!' he said under his breath. But he strode across the room to the window and banged it shut, making the silence suddenly overpowering.

Elizabeth held her breath still, hoping they would go away.

The light flicked off again, and the door closed. Elizabeth's heart pulsated with relief. But she didn't move.

'It must have been Mrs Bayliss,' Abigail was saying outside in the corridor. 'You know how she always listens to everything. She gives me the creeps, Mark. Why don't you get rid of her?'

The table was turned upright, Elizabeth heard the music box wind down and then the lid was shut. She heard the metallic thud as it was set back on the mahogany table.

'Shut up, Abigail,' Mark muttered under his breath, and then Elizabeth heard their footsteps move away down the corridor, still talking in low voices.

It wasn't until the corridor was silent again that Elizabeth relaxed. Her legs were shaking, her hands trembling. Going out of the library, she tried to pull herself together as she made her way back to try and find the drawing room.

'Just like you killed . . .' Abigail had said, and the words spun in her mind, making her throat clench with shock. Just a figure of speech? It *had* to be. Abigail couldn't possibly be saying that Mark Blackthorne was a murderer? Her eyes closed on stinging tears and she swallowed. It was not possible. She wouldn't—couldn't—believe it.

Desperately trying to push the words out of her mind, she felt them come back to her again and again. A tear escaped from her eyes and she felt it trickle saltily down her cheek to the corner of her mouth. She blinked hard, then hard again. To cry was to believe, and she must not believe. She was in love with Mark—she wanted to marry him. How could she justify marrying a man who she thought might be a murderer? How could she justify staying with him? The thought nearly drove her crazy, and she fought away the anxiety with determination. Tonight, after dinner, she would ask him. She would ask him just what was going on. What was in the West Wing? What secret lay hidden behind the locked door? And who were all the others? Reaching the main hall, she rested her head against the wall. The house had now taken on an ominous atmosphere, and she looked up again to see the self-same chandelier tinkling softly in the wind, only this time the lilting gentle sound seemed to be mocking laughter. This house held many secrets. Elizabeth stared at the teasing, sinister chandelier with frightened eyes for a moment, and hated herself for being so susceptible. It was only cut-glass, for heaven's sake. That glittering gold and crystal wasn't human, it couldn't mock her. But all the same, she walked quickly away from it, and almost felt as though it watched her go, laughing softly to itself.

CHAPTER FIVE

THE nightmare engulfed her in a wave of blackness, terrifying images flickering through her mind, demonic faces and icy fear. She felt the wet grass beneath her knees as she knelt at the tomb, saw the dark crosses loom all around her, circling her, threatening her in the icy graveyard. A face appeared behind a cold white tombstone, with blue eyes and sharp white teeth glinting as the moon slipped out above her head. He carried a ball of light. It shone, white and blinding in his hand, and Elizabeth reached out for it. He threw the light, it bounced past her, rolled into a grave, and she looked down in despair, realising that she was naked, her slender body washed in moonlight. She opened her mouth to scream, but it was like drowning, and slow motion took over as she saw him advance on her, teeth bared in a predatory smile. The moonlight flashed on a silver knife blade in his hand, her eyes stretched almost to bursting in terror; she opened her mouth and through the drowning blackness heard a high piercing scream.

Elizabeth jack-knifed upwards in bed, her heart thudding crazily. Her skin was wet with perspiration, her flimsy nightdress clinging to her heated body.

Just a dream! she thought, breathing hard, then her lids closed limply as she remembered the conversation she had overheard last night. Just a dream? she thought then, trying to calm her hammering pulses. She sighed, trembling, and took deep breaths, lying back against the soft goose-feather pillows.

It was stupid to be so worried. Abigail and Mark had been very relaxed with each other last night. Admittedly, at the start of the evening, there had been an edge of tension between them. But Christmas Eve had ended with them all sitting around the fire eating hot mince pies with brandy butter, and drinking fine Napoleon brandy.

Elizabeth had tried to push the frightening conversation from her mind, tried to force it away, but she had been deeply disturbed by what she had overheard. It had pushed back insistently from the edge of her subconscious—her dream was proof of that. It would haunt her until she unravelled it, she knew that. The subconscious is a funny thing, she thought, feeling tears prick her eyes; it just won't let you ignore danger. Almost like an alarm, it had been shouting at her, flashing red lights crazily as a warning.

Suddenly she stiffened. The door clicked open. She froze in the bed, hearing breathing, then footsteps approaching the bed.

The dark red curtains were pulled back, and Mark looked down at her. 'Elizabeth?' he said softly. 'Are you all right?'

She whitened visibly, and fear leapt in her eyes.

Mark frowned. 'What is it? Why did you scream?' The tenderness in his voice made tears sting her eyes. He was flushed from sleep, his hair ruffled. He wore a short black dressing gown that exposed his chest.

'I had a nightmare,' she told him huskily—and

could have kicked herself immediately she had said it.

'A nightmare?' His eyes glittered as he frowned. 'What about?'

Elizabeth swallowed. 'I can't remember,' she said quickly, and he frowned, so she added, 'I was just frightened, that's all. I woke up frightened, but I can't remember the nightmare.'

Mark studied her for a moment, then said slowly, 'Perhaps it was the storm that frightened you,' and she looked at him for a second, puzzled. Then she heard the howling wind outside, the trees being bent in submission, their leaves rustling noisily.

'Yes,' she said slowly, 'it must have been the storm.'

Mark picked up a box of matches from the table. 'The electricity's failed.' He struck a match, the smell of burning sulphur strong, and held it to the long white candle in the antique silver holder. 'It always fails in a storm,' he told her, and the yellow flame of the candle lit up his features in the darkness of her chamber.

'What time is it?' asked Elizabeth, and Mark looked at his watch.

'Just after three,' he told her. He sat on the edge of the bed, watching her, and said, 'I'll stay with you for a while. Until you feel safe enough to sleep.' He smiled, one hand reaching out to stroke her hair. 'You can't sleep with the candle burning—the curtains would catch fire.'

Elizabeth jumped as she heard the old house creak under the assault of the wind, and Mark frowned, leaning forward.

'Don't be frightened,' he said softly, and his arms slid round her, holding her close. 'I'm here.

I'm with you now.' He stroked the back of her neck with one strong hand, his heart thudding a steady rhythm. Elizabeth clung to him—but not out of fear of the storm. Out of fear of herself and him. The words Abigail had spoken last night kept coming back to her with terrifying clarity, dancing in her mind like flashes of lightning.

Looking up, her eyes desperately sought reassurance. What was hidden in the West Wing? Who were all the others, and what had Abigail meant when she said he had killed? She couldn't ask him. She couldn't admit to eavesdropping—not now that she had been stupid enough to hide in the library afterwards, stupid enough not to mention it to him at dinner.

Mark drew back, animal instincts sensing fear. 'Don't look at me like that,' he said under his breath. 'As though you were accusing me of something!'

The flickering candlelight in the bedchamber lit up that dark face, giving it an unearthly pallor, almost a face from beyond the grave. Elizabeth felt herself draw away from him, her mouth dry. She had to know the answers.

'Mark——' she thought quickly, her eyes intense, wary, 'I heard Abigail talking to her husband tonight, after dinner. She was talking about me—about there being others. What did she mean?'

She felt him tense, staring at her. Did he believe her, she wondered, or would he guess that she had deliberately eavesdropped tonight?

'Others?' he said tonelessly, and his eyes were guarded as he watched her. 'Do you mean other women?'

'You tell me.'

He blinked, and said slowly, 'There have been others—so many I've lost count. And all of them with dark blue eyes and black hair.' His hand stroked her cheek gently. 'But they pale into insignificance beside you. They meant nothing to me.'

Elizabeth swallowed. 'What happened to them?' she asked, her voice low and intent.

He frowned. 'Happened to them?' A smile touched his hard mouth as he drawled lazily, 'You talk as though I'm Bluebeard!'

Elizabeth's blood ran cold. Candlelight played on his hard cheekbones, turning them gold, his cool blue eyes glittering. Mark Blackthorne, a man with power and wealth at his fingertips, a man with a penchant for black-haired women with blue eyes, a man who kept secrets locked behind the doors of the West Wing—a man she was in love with, intended to marry. Am I going mad? she thought crazily.

He was watching her, amused. 'You look quite terrified,' he said softly. 'Do you really think I have a room full of dead women in this house?'

Elizabeth stared, speechless.

His amusement slowly changed to surprise as he frowned. 'Good God,' he muttered in astonishment, 'I do believe you're serious! You silly girl. Nothing happened to them! I should imagine they're all married by now, or on the lookout for someone new.'

But she did not relax. 'Do you love me, Mark?' she asked tensely.

His frown deepened. 'Of course!' he said, staring at her. 'Don't you know that?' But she didn't reply, only lay stiffly in his arms. 'What's happened, Elizabeth?' he asked in a deeply serious tone. 'Why have you begun to doubt me?'

She looked away, biting her lip. 'I hear people talking,' she said softly. 'I'm sure they're talking about me. They watch me as though I'm a ghost, as though they're frightened of me. And this house—it frightens me. It seems to have so many secrets.' She looked back at him through her lashes, hoping he wouldn't guess that she had overheard him in the library.

But he only smiled, and held her close to him, pressing his mouth to her cheek. 'Darling, it's just your imagination. There are no secrets in this house, I can promise you.'

But she felt his heart beating faster than it had been before, and as she looked at his face she saw his eyes staring fixedly above her head as though he was thinking hard about something, something he wouldn't share with her.

Suddenly he drew away from her, holding her shoulders as his eyes sought her face as though for reassurance. 'Elizabeth——' he said deeply, 'you know that if I ever kept secrets from you, it would be for a good reason. You understand that, don't you?'

She frowned, and remained silent.

'And that I would tell you, once the time was right,' he continued carefully. 'That is . . . if there ever were any secrets.'

Was this a plea for her trust? Elizabeth stared at him, unable to deny him that trust if it was. She was getting nowhere fast with this conversation, but she sensed that what she had said had worried Mark for some reason. That, at least, relaxed her. Whatever was locked in the West Wing couldn't be anything very bad. However hard she tried she just could not believe he was a dangerous man. Studying his hard-boned face in the candlelight, she felt her heart skip a beat. My God, I love him too much for my own safety, she thought, suddenly afraid, and closed her eyes to escape the feelings he provoked in her.

Giving him a little smile, she nodded. 'I understand that, Mark. Of course I do.'

He relaxed, a sigh escaping from his tanned throat as he held her tight. 'Good,' he murmured against her hair. 'And you believe that I'm in love with you?'

Running her fingers over the face she loved so badly, she smiled. 'Yes. I just need to hear it occasionally.'

Mark looked at her through hooded lids. As her hand rested on his chest, she heard his heartbeat thud strong and true against her palm. 'I've only been in love once before,' he said in a deep, husky voice. 'It's difficult for me to say it because it goes too deeply. Sometimes it takes my breath away just to look at you, and that's when I most want to say it, but my heart beats like hell every time I start to, so I just close up again.'

Elizabeth stared at him in wonder, her eyes shining. 'Tell me again,' she whispered, and her hand slipped to his neck, stroking his skin.

He laughed huskily. 'Not fair!' he murmured, kissing her slowly. 'Especially not when I'm lying next to you in a very compromising position!'

Elizabeth looked up through her lashes. 'I'm all for being compromised,' she whispered, and he laughed.

'Careful!' He pushed her gently back against the pillows, his breath uneven as he watched her. 'You're playing with dynamite.'

His mouth met hers in a slow burning kiss, and Elizabeth's heart leapt too fast. Exquisite, lingering—she couldn't bear to spoil the tentative kiss by responding too fast. Slipping her arms up to his neck, she slid them gently around him, her fingers touching his black hair.

The kiss deepened with breathtaking delicacy, and his arms drew her closer, his mouth opening hers as he pressed her against him. He murmured her name, and sudden hunger flared between them, making her pulses race out of control as Mark kissed her passionately, his hands sliding down to her waist, tightening with sudden emotion.

He drew away, breathing fast. 'You don't know what this does to me,' he said hoarsely, and bent to brush his lips burningly against her throat. 'I've wanted you so badly it's been driving me crazy. But I thought you preferred it this way. I thought you needed time.'

Elizabeth gasped as his mouth fastened on her throat. 'No,' she whispered, clutching his black head as needles of sexuality shot through her as he sucked gently at her throat, 'I only need you.'

Mark groaned and his fingers slid slowly, carefully to her waist, moving up to her breasts until he pulled her nightdress aside, exposing them to the cool night air. Bending his head, he fastened his mouth on her breasts, sucking hungrily while needles of excitement shot through her again, her legs twining with his.

She had no idea of what she was doing or thinking. She felt only a violent need to touch him, to feel the reassurance of his body after the nightmare, the frightening conversation of last night. Only his flesh would appease her troubled mind.

His fingers slid over her body and he gasped with hunger, his head lifting to look at her, his eyes wild with passion. Slowly, he pulled the nightdress off her, leaving her naked in the pale flickering candlelight while he looked down at her, breathing thickly.

'Elizabeth . . .' He reached out to touch her soft white skin with one shaking hand.

Elizabeth caught her breath on a whimper of desire as he began to tug at the belt of his dressing gown. Her hands slid to his naked chest, stroking him, waiting for him in an agony of hunger.

The door flew open and they both gasped, faces flushed dark red, eyes glittering with shock.

Abigail stood in the doorway. The light from the candelabrum she held flooded in through the open curtains of the bed. Elizabeth felt hot scarlet colour flood over her, and she desperately reached for the covers to pull them over her naked body.

Mark dragged them up over her, his face angry and shocked.

'Elizabeth?' Abigail's voice was dry. 'I thought I heard you scream?'

Mark stared at her, stunned. 'God, you bitch!' he muttered under his breath.

Abigail gave him a pussycat smile. 'So sorry to interrupt your little tête-à-tête,' she said in a honey-sweet voice, and Elizabeth just stared open-mouthed. How could she do something like this? 'But it's late, Mark. Shouldn't you be in your own bed?' She smiled, wide-eyed. 'What are you doing in here?'

'Get out!' Mark grated under his breath.

Abigail just laughed, her black eyes illuminated

by the candelabrum in her hand. 'No wonder you screamed, poor lamb. I'd scream too, if I found him in my bed.'

Mark's jaw clenched angrily. Slowly he got out of the bed, pulling his dressing gown together, jerking the belt tightly at his waist as he stood on the floor, facing his sister.

'So help me, Abigail,' he muttered through his teeth, 'I'll break your neck for this!'

The sloe-eyes laughed at him, and she gave him a slow smile. 'What a nasty temper you've got, Mr Wolf,' she drawled lazily.

'And don't you forget it,' said Mark in a low, biting voice, his whole body tense with anger.

Abigail watched him for a few seconds, then quietly turned and walked away with a little smile, her footsteps soft as she returned to the East Wing where she slept.

Elizabeth stared at Mark. The scene brought back the whole of last night's conversation to her. He obviously thought Abigail had come here deliberately, to break up whatever had been going on between them. The trouble was, Elizabeth had a feeling he was right.

Mark ran a hand through his black hair. 'I apologise for my sister,' he told her. He turned to look at the open door which was now in darkness and thrust his hands into the pockets of his black robe. 'She doesn't know when to mind her own business.'

Elizabeth sat up, hugging the quilt around her knees as she looked at him. 'She said she heard me scream,' she reminded him in a quiet voice. 'Maybe she was worried.'

He gave a harsh crack of laughter. 'She didn't hear you scream,' he said with a snarl. 'She's just being an interfering bitch.' He gave her a quick look, seeing the worry on her face, and smiled, sighing, 'I'm sorry. I'd better go.' He leaned over and dropped a kiss on her mouth. 'Maybe it's better this way.'

Elizabeth curled her hand possessively around his brown throat. 'Why?'

He observed her steadily for a moment. 'Goodnight, Elizabeth.' And he turned and left the room, closing the door behind him.

She watched him go with a mixture of disappointment and sadness—but also anxiety. What on earth was behind all this? Lying back on the goose-feather pillows, she tried to remember every word of that conversation Mark had had with Abigail last night. What had she said to him?—'just like all the others . . .' All the others, Elizabeth thought, and turned over in bed, huddling up like a child as if to protect herself from the truth. How many others had there been? And why were they put into a category like that, as if they—and she—were somehow alike in some way, apart from being in love with Mark Blackthorne?

She curled up tighter, putting her knees into her long nightdress and hugging herself tightly. She had to find out what the mystery was, and soon. She sighed and closed her eyes, trying to sleep. But it was useless. Her mind was locked tightly into Mark, Abigail and the mysteries of this house. It wasn't until four in the morning that she finally slipped into black oblivion.

She woke up early, glancing at her clock, to see it was eight a.m. Trying to get back to sleep, she huddled into the blankets, but it was useless. She got out of bed, showered and dressed, and went downstairs to find the house silent as a tomb.

Mrs Bayliss was up and about. She eyed Elizabeth as she walked along the corridor towards the drawing room.

'There's nobody up yet,' the old woman told her, her eyes cold. 'It's too early for them. There'll be no breakfast till nine.'

Elizabeth nodded, disappointed. She had hoped someone would be around. 'Thank you, Mrs Bayliss.' She wondered what on earth to do in the meantime, then an idea came into her head. 'Oh, is there a piano anywhere in the house?' She smiled nervously. 'I'd like to practise my scales.'

Mrs Bayliss looked at her as though she was mad. 'Aye, there's the old grand in the second drawing room. You'll find it near the library.' She watched her grimly. 'I suppose you'll be wanting to know where that is too?'

Elizabeth shook her head, her face cool. 'No,' she said slowly, 'I know where the library is.' She turned, thanking the housekeeper, and walked towards the main hall, going along the right-hand corridor exactly as she had last night.

The grand piano dominated the big room, which had very little other furniture in it. Elizabeth closed the door and went over to it, flexing her fingers as she rested them on the keys, and started to play an octave, singing with it, opening her vocal chords. Nicky would only nag if she didn't keep up her scales, and she didn't want her voice to close up in the future.

Frowning with concentration, she closed her eyes, pushing her voice higher and higher as she tried to make each note as pure and clear as possible. After fifteen minutes of working, a knock on the door startled her, making her jump.

Abigail came into the room, brows lifted with surprise. 'Oh, it's you!' she said drily, resting her hand on the door. 'I wondered what that racket was.'

Elizabeth closed the piano lid. 'Thanks!' she said, smiling a little, but not meeting the other woman's eyes as memories of last night clouded her mind.

Abigail studied her silently, then said, 'Sorry about last night. It wasn't intentional.'

Elizabeth nodded, looking at the shiny ebony wood of the grand piano. 'That's okay,' she said huskily.

Abigail studied her. 'Anyway—I came to tell you breakfast is ready in the dining room. Mark's waiting for you there.' She watched as Elizabeth got up and went over to the door, still not looking at her. 'He looked in on you ten minutes ago and thought you'd done a disappearing act. He was quite frantic, poor soul.'

They walked quickly to the dining room where Mark was waiting, standing by the window, his lean body tense as he scoured the grounds. He turned as they came in.

'Elizabeth!' The blue eyes pierced her. 'Where were you? I was worried.'

She smiled. 'In the second drawing room.' She went over to him, and stood on tiptoe to kiss his cheek. 'Practising my scales.'

He sighed, bending his head to brush his mouth against hers. 'It didn't occur to me.' He seated her at the table, next to himself, and poured her some coffee from the silver pot on the table. 'We're going riding later—after we've opened the presents.'

Abigail sat opposite them, next to Jim, who was forking fried egg into his mouth at a rate of knots. A healthy appetite, thought Elizabeth, spooning a few kidneys on to her plate.

'Mark loves presents,' Abigail told her, biting into a slice of toast. 'They positively burn a hole in his pocket. He always wants to open them immediately, don't you, dear?'

Mark raised his brows. 'I don't see what's unusual about that. It is Christmas, after all.'

Abigail laughed. 'The difference between men and boys is the size of their toys,' she teased, and Mark gave her an offended look, but ignored her.

After breakfast they went into the drawing room where the big Christmas tree glittered with tinsel and pretty coloured ornaments. Beneath its sparkling branches lay a host of presents wrapped in gaily patterned paper, and they all sat around it while Mark busily handed out presents to everyone.

'Why do you always elect yourself as Santa Claus?' asked Abigail as he handed her an enormous present which was obviously a painting, and Mark ignored her, going over to Elizabeth with her present.

Elizabeth opened it, pulling off the wrapping paper to find a jeweller's box with a Bond Street label embossed in gold on the black velvet. Slowly she lifted the lid—and caught her breath as she saw what it was.

A ruby choker glittered against the black velvet, the stones blood-red, perfect, exquisitely made.

'I can't accept this,' she said huskily. 'It's too much.'

Mark frowned, taking the choker from its box.

'Put it on,' he said deeply, and laid it against her white exposed throat, cold and hard, clipping it at the back of her neck.

Silence suddenly descended in the room. Abigail was staring, frozen, her black eyes wide with what looked like terror.

Mark studied Elizabeth with intense eyes, searching her face for something she didn't understand. 'It's beautiful,' he said finally, his voice intense, and leaned over to kiss her.

Abigail and Jim exchanged shocked glances, but said nothing. Mark took the choker from around her neck and laid it back in the box, and they continued to unwrap their presents. When they had finished, Abigail took Elizabeth upstairs and lent her some riding clothes which luckily fitted her, and she came back down ten minutes later to find that they had all gone to the stables.

She walked to the stables alone, shivering a little in the chill December sunlight. The house and grounds looked magnificent, the grass dewed and gleaming, the fine mist still clinging to the skyline beyond the estate. Elizabeth heard the cold sound of her boots ringing on the cobbled path that led to the stables.

Jim and Abigail were waiting in the doorway as she approached. 'Mark won't be a minute,' said Abigail. 'He's probably still looking at all his presents, the big booby.'

Elizabeth laughed. 'I don't think he'd appreciate that description, somehow!'

Abigail's brows rose. 'No, and it's not really very true. He can be an absolute bastard when he wants to.' She handed Elizabeth a hard hat. 'Here, put this on—it should fit.'

Jim led out a slender bay mare, her heels clip-clopping on the cobbled courtyard, head nodding indifferently. 'I thought Coriander would be a good mount for Elizabeth,' he said.

Abigail looked at the horse for a long moment, then she said slowly, 'No. No, put her on Sultan.'

Jim's draw dropped open like a visor. 'Sultan?' he echoed incredulously. 'Do you think that's wise?'

Abigail nodded. 'I think that's very wise.' But her eyes locked into her husband's defiantly, and Elizabeth frowned as she watched Jim turn, shrugging to take the horse back to its paddock. A few minutes later he reappeared.

A black Arab stallion walked with arrogant grace into the sunlight, his coat glistening like silk, his flanks rippling with supple muscle. Elizabeth stared up at the magnificent creature for a moment, then Abigail said, 'I'll give you a hand up,' and waited to help her on. Elizabeth gripped the thoroughbred's mane and jumped on. Sultan began to dance elegantly, hooves clipping on the cobbled courtyard. Elizabeth took the reins and steadied him until he stopped, shaking his head while she bent to pat his well-muscled neck.

Abigail and Jim mounted their own horses, and Elizabeth felt the uneasiness cloy at her stomach. Jim was giving his wife urgent looks, which were being deliberately ignored.

She nudged the stallion into a walk as they moved away from the stables to the front of the house. As they started up the drive she saw Mark's face at a downstairs window.

A few seconds later the iron door was wrenched open and Mark came out, his face blazing with temper, dressed in riding clothes which made him look wild and incredibly sexy.

'Here comes trouble!' drawled Abigail with amusement.

'I wish you hadn't done this, dear,' Jim muttered unhappily as they reined their mounts to a standstill.

Elizabeth's heart beat faster. She reined Sultan as Mark reached her. He stared up at her, eyes darkly intense.

'Who gave you Sultan?' he asked under his breath.

Elizabeth glanced silently at Abigail.

His black head turned to his sister. 'Your work?' he said in a low, angry voice.

Abigail smiled slowly. 'My work,' she agreed.

His mouth hardened. 'I should have known!' He looked back at Elizabeth. 'Take him back to the stables.'

Elizabeth stared in confusion. Sultan sensed weakness and began to dance nervously, his tail swishing, his eyes staring arrogantly at Mark. Elizabeth tried to stop him, but Mark had already moved.

His hands gripped the reins. 'Get off,' he said tightly, and Abigail leant forward to interrupt.

'Can't you control your temper, for God's sake?' she asked irritably.

Mark ignored his sister. 'I want this horse back in the stables,' he told Elizabeth, his voice taut with anger. 'I don't want him ridden.'

'It wasn't her fault, Mark,' Abigail interrupted again. 'Don't take it out on her——'

Mark turned on her, his upper lip curled in a snarl. 'You poisonous little bitch!' he bit out. 'Haven't you done enough damage? Can't you ever mind your own business?'

Sultan reared. His front hooves started to lift

off the ground as he neighed, and Elizabeth watched in horrified slow motion as the world began to blur with the sudden fast movement. Mark moved faster, though. He yanked the bit hard, and the horse stopped, but refused to settle.

'Get off him,' he said tightly, and Elizabeth slid off the horse with relief, her legs shaking. Mark put his foot in the stirrup and swung on to the horse's back himself. Sultan tried to dance, but was stopped ruthlessly by Mark, who made it very plain who was in control.

He looked down at Elizabeth. 'This horse is dangerous. He's temperamental.' He gave his sister a bitingly angry look. 'Abigail should have had more sense!' Abigail flushed crimson and fell silent.

Mark turned the horse and nudged it with powerful thighs, bending into its neck as it moved away at a fast canter. He looked perfectly matched with the powerful stallion; horse and rider both dark and untameable.

Elizabeth turned to Abigail with incredulous eyes. 'Why did you do it?' she asked slowly. 'Why did you give me Sultan when you knew he was dangerous?'

'I forgot,' snapped Abigail, her face bitterly angry. She looked at Jim, who merely raised his brows and sighed, then she nudged her horse into a trot and went off with Jim following her.

Elizabeth watched them ride away from the house, and felt suddenly very lonely in front of the big house. It seemed to watch her, mocking her in the same way she had felt the chandelier laughing at her last night. The tall grey turrets spiked the sky, long shadows beginning to fall across her face.

She sighed and went inside, going to her room to change. She could not believe Abigail had deliberately given her a dangerous horse. Yet what other explanation was there for Mark's fierce anger? Okay, the horse was obviously valuable—but that wouldn't explain his reaction to his sister.

Sitting down on the edge of her bed, she felt very confused and unhappy. Christmas Day was more or less ruined. Her wedding was only a week away. Mark became more shrouded in mystery the longer she knew him. She wanted to cry, but instead she just stared blankly at the floor and hoped desperately that it would be all right once they were married.

But what if it isn't? a little voice asked inside her, and she closed her eyes, trying to block out the instant doubt that rose up inside her. What if it just gets worse? she thought, eyes tightly shut against the nagging worry.

That was a chance she just had to take. She was too deeply involved with him now to pull out. Only a week, she thought, trying to be more positive about it all. Only one more week and then I'll be his wife, and he'll tell me all about the West Wing, and the secrets that hid in this house.

She heard him come in, heard the front door slam, heard his footsteps approach as he came up the corridor. Elizabeth squared her shoulders and resolved to be optimistic. What choice did she have?

CHAPTER SIX

ELIZABETH glanced across at Nicky in the open carriage beside her. The cool January sunshine shone in her eyes as they clip-clopped their way to the church, the two white horses harnessed with gold-studded leather, white plumes on their proud heads. For a moment, she wished Nicky was her father, and the thought made her lips part with sudden sadness. Then she thought of Mark, and the sadness became a smile as she realised that Mark had come to mean everything to her. At last she could let her father's memory slip away with fondness rather than regret.

'Nervous?' Nicky caught her eye.

She smiled, shaking her head.

His brows rose. 'Then why are you strangling those flowers?'

Elizabeth looked down at the fragile white lilies of her bouquet, and realised she was crushing the delicate stems. 'That's not nerves!' she told Nicky, releasing her tight hold. 'I'm just excited.'

'Excited?' Nicky shook his head. 'I can remember you telling me you wouldn't get married until you were famous!' He folded his arms, grinning. 'You phoney!'

She laughed. 'You know what your trouble is? You believe everything I say!'

The small village church came into view as they turned the corner. People were waiting outside—one or two photographers leaned on the little stone gates, and looked up as the carriage came into view. Elizabeth saw Jeremy and Melanie talking outside the small arched doorway. Jeremy looked smart for once—he was even wearing a tie and carnation.

'You can always change your mind, you know!' Nicky whispered beside her, and she looked at him in amazement, only to see he was grinning, a teasing light in his eyes.

'Are you kidding?' she said softly, and he studied her for a moment, then smiled.

'You really are in love with the guy, aren't you?' he said deeply, and shook his head. 'Why couldn't you have fallen for a guitarist? Much better business sense!'

The carriage stopped, the horses waiting patiently at the church gates. The photographers came forward, faces eager as they aimed their cameras at her. Nicky opened the carriage door and let the steps down, then got out to turn and help her down, holding her hand.

She stepped out, her long white lace dress fluttering in the breeze. Through the lace veil over her face, she saw everything through a fragmented white haze as it fluttered in the breeze. Then scooping her long train with one hand, she slipped her arm through Nicky's and walked along the little path through the grass towards the church.

Jeremy and Melanie waved at her and disappeared into the church, walking quickly up the aisle to take their places. Elizabeth stopped in the doorway, her heart beating fast as the organ music started.

Mark's dark head turned at the first strains of music, and their eyes met across the crowded wooden pews of the church. Elizabeth started to

walk up the aisle, her fingers clutching Nicky's
grey sleeve.

As she joined him, Nicky stood to one side, and
Mark stepped into the centre of the aisle beside
her. Their eyes met again, and she saw a flicker of
a smile as they turned to the priest, who began
booming the wedding ceremony in deep tones. As
she repeated the vows, she felt her heart move
with the reality of what she was saying. Mark's
deep voice beside her as he repeated his vows
made her eyes mist with tears.

His strong tanned hand took her pale fingers
and he slid a thick platinum band on to her
engagement finger. It sparkled in the dim
sunshine which shone through the stained glass
window above their heads.

Afterwards, they walked out of the arched
doorway into the churchyard and posed for
photographs. Elizabeth clung to Mark's arm as
they stood in the January sunshine, and he smiled
down at her.

'Hallo, Mrs Blackthorne,' he drawled lightly in
her ear. His dark head was bent, his black hair
clean and freshly washed. Elizabeth smiled up at
him as he bent to kiss her, and her arms wound
round his strong neck. A cheer went up from the
crowd of friends and relations.

'Surprise!' Jeremy's bright voice beside them
was followed by a boxful of coloured rice-paper
being tipped over their heads, making them break
apart, laughing as they brushed the confetti from
eyes and mouth.

'You pest!' scolded Elizabeth, delighted with
Jeremy's antics. He grinned at her, golden and
cherubic in the sunlight, impish lights in his eyes.

Mark was laughing too, taking rice paper from

his tongue with long fingers. 'Let's get out of here!' he said, taking her hand and running to the carriage. He helped her up and got in, shutting the little door and sitting beside her.

'Bouquet! Bouquet!' shouted Melanie beside the carriage.

Even Abigail looked cheerful, standing hand in hand with Jim at the stone gates, smiling as they both watched Elizabeth and Mark waving from the open carriage.

Elizabeth threw the bouquet and watched the white lilies sail through the air, long blue ribbon fluttering in the breeze from the stems.

'I'm doomed!' Jeremy wailed as the bouquet landed in his hands.

The carriage clicked and rolled away, the horses clip-clopping on the country road while the big wooden wheels spun. 'Who *is* that little goblin?' asked Mark as they waved until they turned the corner and were out of sight.

'Jeremy?' Elizabeth smiled. 'Oh, he's an old friend. He's a songwriter—all his songs are very original, just like him.'

Mark laughed. 'The mind positively boggles!' He slipped his arm around her as they headed towards Carthax House. 'Do you mind very much about not having a honeymoon yet?' he asked, kissing the top of her head.

'It can wait.' She wasn't too keen on spending too much time at Carthax, but now that she was married to Mark, all her fears had disappeared.

He stroked her head where it lay on his broad shoulder. 'I just can't trust those idiots to crack the whip. Nobody's in the mood for work after Christmas and the New Year. They'd all spend their time swanning off to heavy lunches.' He gave her an amused glance. 'Nothing would get done.'

'You can hardly blame them,' she pointed out, dimpling.

'Oh no?' he drawled lightly.

Elizabeth laughed. 'I'm glad I don't work for you! Are you very tyrannical?'

'Very,' he drawled, his eyes teasing.

Carthax House came into view and they rode along the hedgeways that bordered the estate, turning into the massive gates and starting up the driveway. The great house loomed up before them, all turrets and spikes, looking today like a fairytale castle instead of a haunted mansion.

Elizabeth brightened. The wedding had definitely taken away her fear of the house and its mysterious secret. She was sure now that Mark would tell her, when he was ready. It couldn't be all that bad, anyway, because she was convinced that he loved her.

The guests were already arriving, and a long line of cars curved the circular driveway. But the carriage had enough room to deposit them at the massive oak doors, and Elizabeth walked to the door with Mark, listening to the chatter of people which came from the house through the open doors.

'Elizabeth?' Mark stopped her at the doorway, and smiled suddenly, swinging her up into his arms and carrying her over the threshold, saying, 'You may not be very traditional, but I am!'

Elizabeth wound her arms round his neck, smiling. 'I like old-fashioned people.'

He grimaced. 'I don't like the sound of that. It makes me feel ancient.'

'You are ancient,' drawled Abigail from the

doorway, and they both turned to look at her in surprise as she stood watching them, a glass of champagne held in her slender white hand.

Mark set Elizabeth slowly back on her feet. 'Put the caustic wit back in its caustic little box, Abigail,' he said irritably. 'Even you can't spoil today.'

Abigail made a face. 'You seem to have left your sense of humour in your other suit, Mark dear.' She came over to Elizabeth and gave her a peck on the cheek. 'Welcome to the family at last.' She gave her a wicked smile and added, 'You poor thing.'

'Thank you, Abigail,' drawled Mark, 'for your kind words. Now push off.'

They went in to the reception room and were greeted with cheers as they went to the carefully arranged long table at the head of the room beneath the minstrels' gallery. A delicate white cake in five tiers stood in the centre of the table with a little bride and groom standing in a twined arch of white roses.

Speeches were made, presents opened, and telegrams read. Elizabeth felt all the worries of the last few weeks slip away from her shoulders as she danced with Mark at the end of the evening, her long white dress caught in the spotlight, Mark's arms around her as they circled the floor, their audience captivated.

Mark smiled as the last strains of music faded away and applause broke out. Slowly he bent his head to kiss her, his mouth warm on hers. A sigh went up from their audience, and Elizabeth's heart beat faster as she twined her arms around his strong neck, intensely proud of her new husband.

'Sir, you can't go in there——' The butler's voice broke into the sudden silence as footsteps hurried towards the Grand Hall.

The front door was slammed, and two black-tailed servants sprang to the doorway, trying to block a man's entry. But he pushed past them, standing in a black evening suit, his collar askew, hair ruffled.

Elizabeth turned her head, still in Mark's arms, to look across at the stranger. As their eyes met she saw his blue eyes widen, an expression of frozen disbelief come over his face as he stared back at her.

'My God!' the man whispered into the sudden silence. 'It's true, then. What they're saying is true!'

Mark tensed, and she shot a frightened look at him to see that his face was cold, expressionless. A mask had slipped down over his arrogant features as he, too, stared at the dishevelled stranger.

'Get Mr Fairhaven a drink,' he said coldly, not moving, and the butler quickly picked up a glass of champagne and took it to the stranger, his footsteps echoing in the silent hall.

But the man Fairhaven brushed the butler aside. 'I don't want a drink.' He came towards them, walking as if drunk, but his blue eyes were piercingly sober, and Elizabeth felt fear ripple icily up her spine. Mark released her slowly. The light from the overhead chandelier shone on Fairhaven's pale brown hair as he stopped dead in front of them, swaying, staring at her.

Mark looked down at him with cold hard eyes. 'We'll talk in the study,' he said in an undertone, so that no one save Elizabeth could possibly have heard.

Fairhaven stared at him for a moment, then back at Elizabeth. He was silent for a moment, while Mark watched him intently. Then he nodded. 'Yes, of course.'

Mark relaxed a little, taking the man's arm and leading him away across the hall. Elizabeth watched them go, her eyes wide with alarm. Then she realised that everyone was staring at her in shocked silence, and hot colour flooded her face.

She gave a ghostly pretence of a smile, and motioned for the music to begin again, walking across to the corner where her friends stood watching and hoping that no one would question her too closely about the incident. People began talking again, drifting on to the floor with their partners to dance. Polite society always won through in the end. They would talk, but not many people would dare question her.

Melanie, however, being her sister, had no such polite barriers. 'What the hell was all that about?' she whispered frantically as Elizabeth joined the little circle of Mayfield inhabitants.

Elizabeth took a glass of champagne and downed it in one gulp, then wished she hadn't. 'I really don't know,' she said coolly, hands twirling the long-stemmed glass restlessly. 'Nothing important, I'm sure.'

Melanie eyed her in disbelief. 'You can lie to me if you like,' she said slowly, 'but for God's sake don't lie to yourself.'

Elizabeth flushed hotly, looking down at the floor. She wished desperately that she was in the study with Mark and the mysterious Mr Fairhaven, could hear what they were saying. Then her mouth firmed with anger and unhappiness. Mark should tell her what was going on. Why didn't he ever tell her?

Mark did not return to the Grand Hall for another half an hour. She spent her time while he was away talking politely to the guests, playing the radiant bride, while all the time tension and fear ate away at her stomach, making her nervous and jumpy. When he finally did reappear, he said nothing about the man Fairhaven, who had disappeared into thin air, merely kissed her on the cheek and smiled, his usual charming self, and danced with her again while the guests gossiped hotly.

The party broke up at around midnight, the witching hour, and the last car drove away from Carthax House, leaving the pair of them standing alone in the doorway, looking out beneath the blue-white light over the doors into the darkness of the Essex winter night.

The tall grandfather clock in the hallway chimed into the silence. It started to strike twelve as Mark turned Elizabeth in his arms and looked down at her with a little smile.

'Bedtime,' he murmured, and she looked at him unhappily.

He started to bend his head to kiss her, but she pushed him away. 'Who's Mr Fairhaven?' she blurted out in one quick hot rush. 'What was he doing here? Why was he staring at me like that?'

Mark was silent for a moment. 'Did it upset you that much?' he asked quietly.

She nodded, uneasy.

He studied her for a long moment, then sighed, sliding his hands into the pockets of his dress suit. Turning, he looked away from her, standing with his back to her for a few seconds. Elizabeth looked at the back of his black head and wondered what on earth was going on.

'Must you know now?' he asked deeply. 'It isn't important. Can't it wait?'

Her eyes flared. 'No, it can't wait!' She felt hot tears begin to sting her eyes. Her wedding day was ruined now, her husband a distant stranger. 'I think I've waited long enough. I know there's some kind of secret you're keeping from me, Mark. You've got to tell me——'

He spun, eyes narrowed. 'Secret?' he asked under his breath. 'What the hell are you talking about?'

'Don't try to talk me out of it,' she said painfully. 'There's some kind of secret in this house, I know there is . . .'

Mark gripped her shoulders, his eyes intense. 'What do you think it is, Elizabeth? You tell me.'

Elizabeth froze, silenced. She saw something frightening in those fierce blue eyes, even though he was cool and controlled, and it made her stare at him in disbelief. Was he threatening her, subtly? She couldn't believe it was happening to her, not now, not on her wedding day. Tears burnt in her eyes, and one slid down over her lashes, running across her cheek to the corner of her mouth.

Mark watched it with slowly changing eyes. His hands bit into her shoulders, making her gasp and back away from him, suddenly afraid.

He looked at her quickly. 'I'm sorry,' he said slowly, and his hands relaxed, sliding away from her shoulders. 'I didn't mean to hurt you—God knows, I've never intended that.'

Elizabeth looked at him, her heart hurting. 'What *is* it, Mark?' she whispered. 'Why won't you tell me?'

He raked a hand through his hair. 'Fairhaven? He's just an old friend of the family.' His mouth moved in a grim smile. 'Come to pay his respects.'

She frowned, her eyes wary. 'Then why did he react like that when he saw me?' she asked in a slow voice.

Mark flicked black lashes, sending his gaze skimming back to her. 'He likes to make an entrance,' he said drily. 'He also likes to upset people. There's no love lost between us. He came here to try and spoil my wedding.'

Elizabeth stared, appalled. 'How horrible!'

He shrugged broad shoulders. 'I told you it wasn't important.' He watched her with hooded eyes. 'I didn't realise it had upset you so much.'

She bit her lip, unsure of whether she even believed him or not. Staring at him, she asked herself if it was quite sane to marry a man she didn't trust as much as she should. But how could she go back now? Would she even want to? that was the real question. And she knew the answer to that already. She wouldn't leave Mark if it was at all feasible to stay with him; she was in too deep now.

Mark sighed, stepping towards her. He slid his arms round her, cradling her against his lean body. 'Darling,' he murmured, 'don't look at me like that. Don't let him spoil it for us. Don't let any of them spoil it for us.'

Elizabeth rested her head on his warm shoulder. 'Why do they want to, though? I don't understand it.'

He stroked her hair. 'Neither do I,' he muttered against her face. 'I wish I did.' He kissed her cheek with warm lips, his long fingers stroking her neck. 'But all you can do is just try to forget it, put it out of your mind.'

She nodded, holding him close. He was right, of course. There was no other course of action for either of them. She loved Mark too much to leave him, and it was perfectly clear that he wasn't going to tell her about the secret he kept hidden in the West Wing—not yet, anyway. All she could do was trust him and stay with him, hoping he would eventually tell her about it.

He took her hand and pressed it to his mouth, then led her over to the stairs as the clock chimed the quarter hour. Climbing the stairs with him, she hoped that he would tell her soon.

Rain woke her, splattering heavily on the windowpanes, the wind howling violently all around the old house, trees bending in submission, branches scraping against the downstairs windows. Elizabeth opened her eyes slowly, lying in the warmth of her big fourposter bed, the covers soft against her naked skin as she stretched like a well-fed cat.

Suddenly she remembered. Her eyes flicked to the man beside her, and her heart beat faster as she looked at his naked spine curved just above the sheets where he lay close to her, huddled up in the blankets. A smile curved her mouth with tenderness. His black hair was ruffled and untidy, stark against the white pillows.

Slowly she reached out one hand to stroke his head, her fingers gentle as she touched his thick black hair. He stirred, frowning, his mouth moving a little as he huddled deeper into the blankets, and Elizabeth smiled again, watching him. His arm moved as he groaned in his sleep, and he slid his hand round her waist, cuddling up to her.

Elizabeth cradled his strong dark head against her breast. At first last night, she hadn't been sure he was actually going to make love to her. He had been so subtle, so teasing as they came into the bedroom. It had been an hour before he finally pushed her back against the pillows and slid her clothes off one by one, his hands burningly sensual as he touched her naked skin. His kisses had deepened, probing her mouth while he stroked her, making her feel as though her bones were liquid, her body on fire. He had quickly stripped himself while she lay watching, and come back to her, twisting together naked while his hands and mouth travelled over her naked flesh, becoming more urgent, more passionate until he finally took her with a wild cry, his voice hoarse as he drove into her, his body meeting hers until the urgency overtook them and they fell together, covered in sweat, each crying out with fulfilment.

She shivered now, feeling the heat suffuse her as she lay next to him, skin against skin in the big fourposter bed. Mark stirred, black lashes flickering, and she looked down at him.

He opened his eyes, then quickly looked up at her, as if to reassure himself that she was still there.

Elizabeth smiled down at him. Their eyes met and held for a few seconds in silence, the only sounds that of the rain battering the lattice window, the wind howling outside.

'Awake at last?' she said softly.

'I had a long night,' he murmured, smiling.

Elizabeth's smile broadened, lights dancing in her blue eyes. 'Indeed?'

His brows rose. 'I was speaking on a purely spiritual level,' he said with dignity, then suddenly he grinned, shifting up in bed to swing his arm around her, pulling her close to his side. 'Did you sleep well?' he asked.

'Of course!' She had slept soundly, exhausted after their lovemaking and the long conversation which had followed, continuing into the early hours of the morning as they lay in each other's arms. 'How about you?'

He laughed deeply. 'Are you kidding?' He kissed the top of her head with warm lips. 'We must do this more often! I've decided I definitely like being married to you. Especially since you look so radiant first thing in the morning.' He smiled, then said suddenly, 'What do you want to do today?'

She turned, surprised. 'I thought you were working?'

He made a face. 'They can do without me for one day. I'll go in tomorrow and kick them extra hard to make up for it!' He caught Elizabeth's amused expression and his brows shot up. He quickly turned her so that she lay across his chest, head turned up to his face, his arm around her neck in a mock stranglehold. 'That amuses you, does it?' he drawled with a smile.

She laughed. 'Only because I can picture it so vividly!'

'I see,' he drawled, his brows raised. 'Don't you want your husband to be the boss?'

Her gaze dropped to his hard mouth, and she said softly, 'Only after I've given him a run for his money.'

Mark bent his head, his lips touching hers, but he didn't kiss her, only murmured, 'I'll enjoy the battle.'

Elizabeth grinned. 'And I'll let you win.'

He laughed, pinning her to the bed with strong hands while she put up a mock struggle, laughing as he pushed her back against the pillows and lay on top of her, holding her still. Then he slowly bent his head and kissed her slowly, his mouth warm, the pressure increasing, the kiss deepening, until they lay together in a passionate embrace, the only sounds those of the rain outside and their excited breathing inside.

Later, Elizabeth showered alone, not yet used to Mark enough to shower with him. Tomorrow, she decided, she would shower with him, but not yet. She dressed in a slim-fitting white skirt and a pale blue blouse, and went downstairs to have breakfast with him. She was ravenously hungry, she discovered, and Mark watched her with indulgent amusement as she polished off a plate of scrambled eggs on toast followed by two fresh croissants which she dipped into a cup of hot milky coffee.

They spent the morning lazily, sitting together talking in the warm Victorian study downstairs. Elizabeth told Mark about her ambitions in her career, and he listened thoughtfully, but she noticed he was frowning too, and wondered why. They had discussed her singing before, and he had been in favour of it.

In the afternoon, they went riding. Mark saddled Coriander for her, and took a sturdy-looking white thoroughbred gelding for himself. It was still raining, although it had lessened to a fine drizzle, and the grey skies looked as though they might clear.

Wet and cold, they arrived home regenerated after the long ride, their faces pink from exertion, lungs working vigorously, their muscles hot and supple.

'I'm starving!' said Mark, laughing as he put the horses back in their paddocks. Steam rose from the well-muscled bodies of the horses, and he covered them with short blankets as he led them away.

'Me too!' Elizabeth watched from the doorway, then noticed that Sultan's paddock was empty. Frowning, she said slowly, 'Mark—where's Sultan?'

He stiffened, standing still for a moment. 'Sultan?' he said, patting Coriander as he closed the small door on her. 'I sold him.' He looked over his shoulder with hooded eyes. 'Why do you ask?'

Elizabeth watched him with worried eyes. 'Just curious,' she said, seeing the tense set of his dark face.

As they walked back to the house, she looked up at the grey spikes which towered threateningly towards the sky. Her eyes fell on the West Tower, and she glanced at Mark, seeing him look at her guardedly, tapping his riding crop against his black boots.

'There's a storm blowing up,' he commented, assuming she was looking up at the grey sky.

Elizabeth shot him a quick look. 'What's in the West Wing?' she asked, her heart thumping as she tried to make her voice sound casual. 'I've never been in there. Do you keep it locked?'

Mark stared at her for a moment, his step halting. Then he said, 'It's empty,' his voice cool and offhand as he began walking again. 'I keep it locked because there's nothing in there. I can't run the whole house—it would be pointless. It's much too big.'

Elizabeth dropped the subject. They went upstairs to shower and change, and she stepped out of the shower with a thoughtful frown, wrapping herself in a warm dressing gown after she had dried herself. Mark was obviously not ready to tell her. Well, it could wait, she decided, going into the bedroom.

Mark was waiting in the bedroom in front of a newly-lit fire. 'I brought some food up,' he told her, indicating two plates of hot buttered toast, and two pink mugs full of steaming hot chocolate. Elizabeth smiled and went over to sit on the bedroom couch with him.

They talked for hours, but the heat from the fire made her drowsy, and eventually she fell asleep in his arms.

She awoke in darkness. Her neck ached, and she sat up, looking around the room which was lit only by the flickering firelight. Mark was soundly asleep, his dark lashes resting on his tanned cheek as he breathed deeply. Elizabeth carefully got up without waking him.

She tried to put the light on, but it wouldn't work. The storm, she remembered, listening to the newly howling wind and rain. The electricity must have failed again. How annoying! She fumbled in the darkness for a candle, striking a match and lighting it as she went out of the bedroom into the corridor.

She wanted to do her vocal exercises before dinner. But as she started to walk towards the main staircase, her eye was caught by a ghostly reflection of herself in a faded gilt-edged mirror.

My face, she thought, staring into the eerie mirror. Why do people stare at me so? It must be something to do with my face. The candle-flames licked at her features, sharpening and distorting the delicate white skin, fragile bone, big violet eyes and ruby red lips.

What *was* in the West Wing? She glanced over her shoulder. It wasn't far from here; this corridor led to the West Wing. She could just take a quick look before dinner, before she did her vocal exercises. What harm could it do? It couldn't be anything very bad.

The big oak door of the West Wing was closed. Elizabeth held the candle higher, going towards it on soft feet, trying to be as silent as possible. The heavy circular handle was rusty, and she reached out for it, feeling it cold against her fingers.

The door opened heavily, creaking in protest as she swung it back. Heart thumping madly, she looked at the corridor in front of her. Slowly she began to walk along the old, musty corridor, looking anxiously from side to side.

Silver glinted for a second, and she frowned. A door at the end of the corridor—a door with a silver lock. She walked silently towards it, her pulses racing.

'What are you doing in here?'

She spun round, heart leaping with fright. Mrs Bayliss was watching her with cold eyes, and Elizabeth breathed deeply, thankful it wasn't Mark.

'I was exploring,' she said quickly, her breath constricted. 'That's all.'

The old woman nodded her head. 'There's nothing to see here,' she told her grimly, 'The West Wing's been closed these last three years. You'll be better off exploring elsewhere.'

It was difficult for Elizabeth to argue. She

wasn't used to dealing with housekeepers. She
nodded and began to walk away back down the
corridor, away from the room with the silver
lock, away from the secret which lay behind its
polished doors.

Mrs Bayliss followed her, locking the heavy
door to the wing with the set of keys which
jangled from her waist on a long thin chain.

'I'll be serving dinner late, tonight,' she told
her. 'The electricity'll not be back for a while yet.
You'd be well advised to go back to your husband
until the power's on again.'

Elizabeth drew herself up to her full height,
refusing to be ordered around by the woman. 'On
the contrary,' she said as coolly as she could, 'I'm
going downstairs to the music room. I have to
practise my scales.'

Mrs Bayliss raised her straggly grey brows. 'As
you like, madam,' she said with grim amusement.

Elizabeth turned, her lips compressed, and
walked quickly away from her, going down the
central staircase and along the ghostly echoing
passages to the second drawing room where the
piano was.

Sitting down at the polished ebony piano, she
set the candlestick on its lid, seeing the eerie
light reflected in the black wood, yellow and
silver blending in a flickering pattern. Running
her fingers over the keys, she started to play
octave after octave, singing the scales, and extra
vocal exercises until her voice began to open up.

Once her voice had opened, she began to sing
a popular ballad which had become a classic in
recent years, recorded by different artists the
world over. Closing her eyes, she controlled her
voice, singing in clear high tones, allowing the

lyrics to dance like arrows in rich sound above the lilting notes of the piano.

As the song approached its climax, she allowed feeling to take over, but controlled it with effortless technique, her voice soaring with the power of the lyric, rephrasing for more effect, opening her throat up to round the tones. It excited her, hearing her voice rise above the music with such clarity and power.

The door opened suddenly, and she stopped, catching her breath.

Mark stood in the doorway, his face illuminated by the candle he held. 'You're superb,' he said after a long moment. 'I hadn't realised you were this good.'

Closing the door, he came in, still wearing the dark silk dressing gown he had put on after their ride this afternoon.

'I'm glad you liked it,' said Elizabeth, feeling pleased with herself. He had never heard her sing before. She was glad he had heard her when she was in good voice, when atmosphere had helped her voice.

'I liked it too much,' he told her, frowning. 'That's the problem.'

She studied him, at a loss. 'I don't understand . . .' she began slowly.

Mark put his candle on the piano next to hers. 'You have a remarkable talent, Elizabeth. It might take you away from me. I don't think you should continue singing.'

She stared, appalled. 'Don't be silly, Mark!' she said uncertainly. 'We discussed it, and you told me I could continue.'

He watched her through hooded lids. 'I've changed my mind,' he told her bluntly.

She just stared at him, speechless for a moment. Then she stood up, thinking hard. 'You can't stop me,' she said quietly. 'You must know that. Surely you'd rather be with me rather than against me?'

'And lie to myself at the same time?' He shook his black head. 'I can't pretend something I don't feel. And I don't feel happy about your career any more.'

'But why?' she asked hopelessly.

He shoved his hands into the pockets of the black silk robe. 'You're too good,' he said curtly. 'If recognition came, it would be enormous. It would split us eventually—you must see that.'

Elizabeth shook her head angrily. 'No, I don't,' she said, her eyes intent on his face. 'It would only come between us if we let it.'

His mouth firmed into a hard line. 'I'm not going to discuss it any more. It's pointless.' He picked up his candle swiftly, his face angry. 'Just remember that you'll be going against my wishes if you don't give it up.'

'Oh, for God's sake, Mark . . .' she began angrily, but he turned with a harsh expression, saying:

'The discussion is over!' and started to stride over to the door, his shoulders set angrily. As he reached the door he looked over his shoulder at her tight angry face and added, 'By the way, Mrs Bayliss tells me you were in the West Wing tonight. Why?'

Elizabeth floundered, her face colouring. 'I was curious. I wanted to see it.'

'Don't go there again,' he said tightly. 'It's empty. I'll lock it tonight for good.'

The door slammed shut and he was gone,

leaving Elizabeth staring at it with incredulous eyes. She could hardly believe that conversation had taken place. Mark's selfishness about her career was almost beyond belief. At the moment, all her career consisted of was working hard on her voice and recording songs in her sister's house. It was true that Nicky had interested several major record companies in her. It was true that R.C.I. were waiting to hear her new material. But surely he couldn't believe a recording career would split them up, destroy their marriage?

And then there was the business about the West Wing—almost as though he and Mrs Bayliss had joined forces against her. Elizabeth sat down slowly, deeply upset and confused.

What was hidden in the West Wing? She had to find out.

CHAPTER SEVEN

MARK left early the next morning. He got dressed in silence while Elizabeth lay in the bed watching him as he stood in front of the looking glass, tying his tie, his movements quick and brisk. He turned as he shouldered into his black jacket, the waistcoat he wore fitting tightly to his lean waist and hips. He had been silent and brooding all last evening, eating dinner with her in the candlelit dining room without saying a word to her. Elizabeth had been too proud and angry to make the first move in conversation, so they had sat in tense silence while Mrs Bayliss served the dinner. And when they had made love last night it had been with anger and hostility, almost tearing each other's bodies to pieces as they fell together in violent ecstasy, each breathing harshly after the shattering release of tension.

Mark turned now, eyes guarded. 'I may be late home,' he said expressionlessly. 'Don't wait up for me.'

Elizabeth's mouth compressed. Tears clouded her eyes, but she blinked them back angrily and didn't speak. What could she possibly say to him? She had to try to make him understand that she was serious about her career.

He watched her for a moment, then put his watch on, his long fingers nimble, black hairs twining around the silver watch. 'Mrs Bayliss will get your meals,' he said coolly. 'Crane is around somewhere if you want to drive out to see your . . .' he paused, then added sardonically, 'your friends.'

Elizabeth closed her eyes, wishing there was some way of getting through to him. She ought to have spoken to him at dinner last night and ended the hostility.

Mark watched her angrily. 'Well, say something, for God's sake!' he snapped. 'Don't just sit there like a patient saint!'

She glared at him. 'What do you want me to say?'

His mouth compressed. 'God knows,' he said bitingly. 'Anything would be better than watching you sigh and close your eyes like a bloody martyr!'

She gave him an angry look, but said nothing.

There was a tense silence. Then Mark took a set of keys from his pocket, and threw them on the bed. The big hooped ring surrounded by a multitude of keys clattered noisily.

'The keys to the house,' he drawled tightly. 'You are the mistress here, after all.'

Elizabeth held up a large silver key, her heart beating fast. 'What's this one for?' she asked slowly, staring at it.

Mark stiffened. 'It's the key to my private room,' he said under his breath. 'I don't want you to use it.'

She looked at him intently. 'Why not, Mark?' she asked in a low voice.

His blue eyes glittered. 'Just don't use it,' he said coldly.

Elizabeth felt the key burn into her finger. It had to be the one. Hadn't she seen the lock it fitted last night? The polished oak door, the gleaming silver lock, eerie in the candlelight. Her heart beat faster with fear and excitement as she remembered Abigail saying, 'What will she do if she goes to the West Wing? We all know what she'll find there . . .'

She put the keys down on the bed beside her. 'Well,' she said with false calm, 'I'll see you when you get home tonight.'

Mark's eyes flickered, narrowing. 'Yes,' he said slowly, and came towards her, bending to brush cool lips across her cheek. 'We'll discuss your career tonight. Maybe we can come to some arrangement.'

Elizabeth looked at the hard-boned face. 'There's only one possible arrangement, Mark,' she said firmly.

His mouth compressed into a hard line. 'We'll see,' he said curtly, and turned to go out of the bedroom. At the door, he turned, looking at her. 'I'll be home at around eleven or midnight.'

She nodded. 'So you said.'

'Remember——' he said darkly, 'you can use every key on the ring, but not the silver one. Don't go into my private room.'

Elizabeth watched him intently. 'What have you got hidden in there?'

His jaw clenched. 'Don't go into that room,' he said tightly, and went out, slamming the door behind him.

Elizabeth picked up the key ring, gazing at the little silver key.

She spent the day exploring the house, going from room to room with the jangling bunch of keys, finding rooms she hadn't known existed, had always passed by without noticing, but which were now made available to her through the keys of the house.

Mrs Bayliss appeared several times. Is she spying on me, Elizabeth thought, or am I just going paranoid? It seemed too coincidental that Mrs Bayliss would appear just as Elizabeth moved quietly towards the West Wing.

At any rate, she decided to wait until tonight before going to the silver-locked room. It was too risky with Mrs Bayliss around. She was as off-putting as a witch's familiar, hovering silently, cold eyes watchful and ever-present.

Mrs Bayliss was cooking the dinner at seven o'clock, and Elizabeth felt safe enough to creep silently up to the West Wing. The heavy oak door creaked open as she pressed her weight against it and turned the circular handle.

Then she stopped, listening. The house was silent. Mrs Bayliss wouldn't interfere.

The door at the end of the corridor gleamed with sinister invitation. Elizabeth swallowed, staring at the mysterious silver lock, and the engraved silver key in her hand. But she decided not to go in there just yet.

Mark's private room could wait until after dinner, when Mrs Bayliss had gone. Instead, she went to another room in the West Wing, to the left of the other door. Finding the right key, she slipped it into the lock and turned it, pushing the heavy oak door open.

It was dark inside. The heavy velvet curtains were · closed. Flicking on the light switch, Elizabeth stared for a moment in complete surprise at the room that confronted her.

Cobwebs hung from a chandelier in the central ceiling, dust covered the oak dining table in a fine white layer. The chairs and couches around the room were covered by white dust sheets. The dark velvet curtains were yellowed with age and dust.

Elizabeth walked in, running her fingers over the ancient dust and cobwebs. Two candelabra stood at either end of the dinner table, clad in fine white cobweb robes, which she ran her fingers through, breaking them as dust flew silently into the air.

Going to the curtains, she fingered them, then drew them back. One curtain fell to the floor and she jumped, staring at it, heart beating fast from surprise.

What was this room? she asked herself, staring incredulously. Who had lived here previously? Why was it left to decay and rot—as though it was a grave, a room filled with the sickly smell of death?

'Mrs Blackthorne.' A cold voice from the doorway made her spin, heart thumping madly.

She swallowed. 'Yes, Mrs Bayliss?'

The woman watched with a cold, hard face. 'Your dinner is ready,' she said through barely moving lips. 'It's been ready these last ten minutes. And not for want of calling you!'

Elizabeth straightened. 'I've been looking over my new home,' she said, underlining her words with a proprietorial edge.

Mrs Bayliss nodded. 'I'll see to locking this wing up for you,' she told her calmly. 'You go down and eat your meal before it's cold.'

Elizabeth's mouth compressed. Walking to the door, she watched as Mrs Bayliss took her own set of keys and started to close the door behind them with a resounding thud.

'Whose room was that?' she asked with a frown. 'Why is it allowed to decay like that?'

'Mr Blackthorne's orders, madam,' said Mrs Bayliss, but refused to add to that cryptic statement.

Elizabeth went slowly downstairs to the dining room, where her meal waited on a hostess trolley, still hot despite what Mrs Bayliss had said about it getting cold. She ate in an agony of suspense, wanting the housekeeper to go home as soon as possible so that she could return to the West Wing and open the door to Mark's private room. She was convinced that the mystery lay hidden behind that polished oak door, and the silver key would unlock the secret for her.

It was dark now, and Elizabeth stood by the window in the dining room waiting for Mrs Bayliss to leave. Mark would be home in two hours—eleven or midnight, he had said. That left her just enough time to see inside the locked room before he arrived home. Perhaps there was nothing in there after all—but the gripping suspense which held her was too much of a powerful instinct to be ignored. And she was certain that the room was the most important in the house.

'I'll be going home now, madam.' Mrs Bayliss put her head round the door at ten, after delaying it as long as possible, Elizabeth thought.

Elizabeth tried to conceal her excitement. 'Okay,' she said calmly, 'I'll see you in the morning.'

Mrs Bayliss looked anxious for a moment. 'You'll find plenty of books in the library, madam. It should keep you occupied until Mr Blackthorne gets home.'

'Thank you,' Elizabeth said coolly, 'I'll take your advice.'

Mrs Bayliss looked relieved. 'Oh, good,

madam. Doesn't do to find yourself idle when you're alone.' She smiled, amazing Elizabeth, who had never seen her smile before. 'Goodnight, madam.'

Elizabeth watched discreetly from the window as Mrs Bayliss climbed on her bicycle and rode away down the dark drive and off the estate. The minute the bicycle was out of sight, its single red light disappeared, Elizabeth let the curtain drop back into place and ran upstairs to get her set of keys.

The door to the West Wing swung open. Elizabeth hurried to the last door, the silver key clutched in her hand, slipping it into the lock and turning it with a loud click. She held the polished silver handle for a moment, feeling it smooth beneath her fingers, then she pushed it open, and flicked the light switch on.

White dazzled her. A woman's bedroom, perfectly preserved, confronted her. It was immaculate. White silk curtains hung from a large fourposter bed. A white deep-pile carpet covered the floor. A white couch sat next to a big white dressing table. Wardrobes ran along the walls, gold handles glinting under the light.

Silence washed over her like mist in a churchyard. As she walked into the room, thoughts ran like wildfire through her troubled mind. She didn't understand, even now, as she looked around the room in amazement, and the more she didn't understand, the more she had to.

Opening the wardrobes, she stared incredulously. Rows of white dresses—silk, satin, lace—confronted her, along with rows of white fur coats, soft to the touch as she ran her fingers slowly over them.

Going to the dressing table, she stopped dead at what she saw. The jewellery box was open, and rubies cascaded out of it like a waterfall of freshly spilt blood, all glittering under the light from the chandelier overhead.

Someone was watching her. Heart freezing, she stiffened. She swung round, breathing fast to look across at the far wall. It wasn't a person at all. It was a painting.

'My face . . .' she whispered, her fingers going to her cheeks instinctively as she stared at the portrait. Then she walked slowly over to stare up at it.

It was her face, her eyes that stared back at her. Only it wasn't her. The thick black hair was piled high in curly disarray on top of a face that was her double. The enormous violet eyes were shaped identically—yet there was a shallowness there, a certain expression of casual youth, that was not in Elizabeth's own eyes. The girl was laughing, her pretty mouth open in a smile exposing neat white teeth—and, Elizabeth thought, a certain cat-like malice—almost spite, but far too pretty to be that. The pale white skin was almost translucent, like her own, and the high prominent cheekbones were a little sharper.

And around her neck, in blood-red stones, there glittered a choker. It cut her throat, swanlike, pale, and hardened the white fur she wore.

Elizabeth felt shock freeze her mind, and she looked down slowly to the inscription on the painting, in gold, giving the dates of birth and death of this girl who was her twin. She had died three years ago. But her name made Elizabeth's body and heart go first white-hot, then icy cold as realisation dawned.

Katherine Fairhaven-Blackthorne.

Elizabeth caught her breath. His dead wife, she realised with a blank face. Dead, but not yet buried. And she was her living, breathing double. Slowly, she walked over to the bed and sank on to it, her legs weak as she tried to calm herself down.

A photograph in a silver frame was propped on the bedside table, and she stared at it, her mouth thinning into an unhappy, angry line. A wedding photograph of Mark with his arm round this girl, Katherine Fairhaven-Blackthorne, both smiling, confetti in their hair.

Elizabeth could not cry, however badly it hurt to look at the woman in Mark's arms. She felt devoid of all emotion, devoid of all thought. She just sat on the bed, gazing into space with an empty expression, looking back on the past, on her life with Mark so far, and seeing all the loose ends finally come together.

It must have been an hour later that she heard Mark calling her name from downstairs. His footsteps came up to their bedroom, then his voice grew urgent and she could almost hear him thinking as he realised where she was.

He hurried to the doorway, breathless, catching the door-jamb to stop himself. As he gazed at her in the silence, she heard his frantic laboured breathing, saw the fierce blue of his eyes.

He swallowed hard. 'Elizabeth . . .' he said deeply, but she didn't let him speak.

'You're too late,' she said expressionlessly, 'I've already seen her.'

He studied her, his eyes glittering. 'I told you not to come in here. I asked you to keep out of this room. I would have told you eventually—but I didn't want you to find out like this.'

Her face was white, blank. 'Does it make any difference?'

Mark watched her intently. 'I can explain——' he began, but she cut in:

'I'm sure you can!' And it frightened her to hear herself, cold and hard.

He shook his head. 'You don't understand——'

'Oh yes, I do!' she retorted bitterly, as something snapped inside her and the anger was released, white-hot. 'You married me because I looked like your dead wife—Katherine Fairhaven-Blackthorne, back from the grave.' She looked at him, her eyes hating him. 'No wonder everyone stared at me! No wonder Abigail dropped her glass. They were terrified—I must have scared the life out of them!'

Mark took a step towards her, frowning. 'Please, don't hurt yourself. I know what it looks like, but it's not what you think.'

Her heart hurt. 'Don't say any more,' she said in a barely controlled voice. 'I don't want to hear it.'

Standing up, she walked quickly to the door, although Mark followed her, trying to stop her. But Elizabeth couldn't bear to listen to his excuses for another second. It was beginning to hurt, the pain was coming through the layers of protective shock she had hidden in for the last hour. She wanted to fight it, not give in to the pain. It was easier to feel nothing, think nothing.

'Where are you going?' Mark stopped her in the corridor.

'Home,' she said abruptly, 'where I belong.' Walking away from him, she concentrated on nothingness, trying not to allow him to interfere with her calm.

He followed her again, taking her arm as sh
reached the top of the stairs. 'You can't leave,' h
said urgently, 'not without giving me a chance t
explain.'

'Can't I?' she said with hatred, her eyes violet
darkening with anger as she tried to channe
everything she felt into hatred of him. 'Just watch
me!'

Wrenching her arm free, she descended th
stairs. Mark watched her from the top of th
stairs, frozen in disbelief by her angry, hatin
outburst, watching her open the double door
and go out into the night, leaving them ope
while she looked into the black Ferrari, saw th
key and got in. His voice echoed through th
night as she started the car, hearing him call he
name urgently, but she ignored him. Slipping th
keys into the ignition, she started the blac
sports car, hearing the engine roar and throb i
the cold night. The headlights flicked or
illuminating the path ahead, and she started t
pull away and drive off down the drive unde
the light of the blue-white lamp above th
double doors.

Looking in the rearview mirror as she drov
away, she saw Mark standing in the doorway
watching her go. In that moment she hated him
wished she had never met him, hoped she woul
never see him again.

Driving through the dark lanes of Essex, sh
tried to fight the pain inside her. But the tea
began to sting her eyes as she drove, and s
blinked angrily, her chin trembling, tears blurrin
her vision.

With a muffled curse in a weak, broken voic
she pulled over to one side of the road, stoppi

the car until she had recovered enough to drive. A few solitary tears slipped out from her lashes and over her cheeks as she sat staring at the steering wheel.

But after two or three silent tears, the anger returned, and she found herself hating him again. Images of Katherine's bedroom flickered through her mind like a silent film, memories of the silver-framed photograph on the bedside table disturbed her. She thought of her first meeting with Mark, near here, on the road to Mayfield.

She couldn't face thinking about it any more; it was too painful. She allowed emptiness to settle over her like a void, until she felt nothing at all, thought nothing at all. She re-started the Ferrari, and an automatic pilot was now in control. She felt nothing, thought nothing. Emptiness chilled her as she drove towards Mayfield, towards warmth and safety and people who loved her. Their kind words and comforting presence would eventually thaw the numbness she felt.

'How did she die?' Melanie handed her a mug of steaming coffee as she sat cross-legged on the floor in front of the blue-gold flames of the dirty old gas-fire.

Elizabeth shook her head. 'I have no idea.' Staring down blankly at the coffee she cradled in both hands, she added, 'He didn't tell me. Or rather—we didn't get that far.'

Melanie eyed her shrewdly. 'You mean you just walked out on him.'

Elizabeth looked at her sister and nodded. Mayfield was empty tonight, Melanie was all alone. She was grateful for the quiet of the warm, familiar living room—at least she didn't have to explain her problems in front of a lot of people. She was surprised that Mark had not followed her to Mayfield—but then he probably realised that she was too deeply shocked to even react to his presence if he did come. She felt, quite simply, exhausted. If he walked into the room now, she would just look at him blankly. She felt devoid of all feeling.

Melanie went over to the window, pulling the dirty blue curtains back a little. 'Nice car,' she said quietly. 'What are you going to do with it?'

Elizabeth shrugged. 'God knows.'

Melanie watched her for a moment, then let the curtain fall back into place. 'I'll speak to Nicky about it when he gets here. I expect he'd love to drive a nice Ferrari like that. He'll take it back for you.'

Elizabeth turned her head. 'When he gets here?' Her eyes fell on the peeling white alarm clock, upended in the corner of the room like a forgotten doll. 'It's nearly one o'clock.'

Melanie nodded. 'They've gone to a concert at Wembley. They'll be back in an hour or so.'

'Oh.' Elizabeth looked down at her coffee, indifferent to the damp wisps of steam which curled upwards from it, touching her face. The silence comforted her. She stared down at the carpet, seeing the blue-yellow patterns embedded with ash and spilt coffee, where people had casually flicked their cigarettes, missing the ashtray which lay nearby overflowing with dead ends and ash.

Melanie watched her for a moment, then walked quietly over to her and sat next to her cross-legged. 'I hate to be the one to say this,' she told her, 'but you'll have to snap out of this soon

You won't feel better until you've felt worse—if you see what I mean.'

Elizabeth shrugged, silent.

Melanie lit a cigarette, frowning. 'You say the bedroom was perfectly preserved?' she asked, and at Elizabeth's nod continued, 'He must have loved her very much.'

Elizabeth whitened, catching her breath rawly.

'Oh God, I'm sorry!' exclaimed Melanie, looking at her quickly. Then she frowned. 'I don't know, though. At least you felt something for a minute—it brought you out of zombie-land.'

Elizabeth gazed hard at the floor, feeling the first stirrings of pain. Fighting them back, she felt coldness settle over her again, numbness inside. It was easier. She didn't have to think about it this way. Distorted memories didn't flicker through her head of the past, things she had forgotten about, images of Mark and his sister, things they had said, things which only now were beginning to fall into place. She didn't want to face them now. She would face them tomorrow; she would feel stronger tomorrow.

At half past two cars drew up outside, voices lowered in the night as doors slammed and footsteps approached the house. Melanie had already got up when they heard the cars pull up, and was going to the front door just as the bell rang noisily through the house. Elizabeth sat waiting, her heart thumping painfully as she heard Nicky's voice.

'I like the mean machine outside,' he was saying. 'Whose is it?'

Jeremy was with him, and several others. 'When I'm rich . . .' he began but was cut off by noisy laughter from everyone else.

Elizabeth felt the pain start inside her, and she looked towards the door, feeling terribly alone in the quiet little room as their cheerful voices came through the open front door. She heard Melanie take Nicky aside and start talking to him in a lowered voice as they came towards the living room.

Nicky came into the doorway, looking at her with deep concern. 'Liz?' he said gently. 'What is it, baby?'

She felt her lower lip tremble, and tears misted her eyes.

Nicky clucked his tongue anxiously. 'Oh, Liz!' he exclaimed, and came over to her just as she started to stand up clumsily, feeling the tears start to come. 'You silly girl,' he said tenderly.

She went into his arms, holding him tightly. The tears came, flowing hot and fast over her cheeks as he held her silently, stroking her hair and whispering in her ear, comforting her.

The others came in, noisily at first, but stopping short, falling into silence as they saw Elizabeth crying in Nicky's arms.

'What's up?' whispered Jeremy as Melanie came in.

Melanie shooed them all out of the room and quietly closed the peeling white door, leaving them alone together.

Elizabeth clung to Nicky for what seemed hours until the tears finally stopped. He was sitting down on the sofa with her, his strong arm firm as he held her, rocking her gently, letting her cry it all out of her system.

Eventually she lapsed into hiccoughs, her face raw and tear-stained, her eyes red. Nicky drew back, looking down at her face. He smiled gently, stroking her eyes.

'You look like a panda,' he murmured, smiling, 'Your mascara's run all over you!'

Elizabeth hiccoughed, smiling too. 'Oh dear!' She rubbed her eyes, presenting herself for his scrutiny. 'Is that better?'

He laughed under his breath. 'I like pandas!' he told her, then sobered, studying her seriously. 'Do you want to tell me what happened?'

Elizabeth sighed, looking down at her hands. 'I look like his dead wife,' she said bluntly.

Nicky frowned. 'How much like her?'

Elizabeth took a deep breath, muttering, 'I'm her double.'

Nicky stared, incredulous. He took a packet of cigarettes from his pocket and lit one, taking the lighter from his denim jacket. 'I didn't even know he'd been married before.'

'Neither did I!' She glanced at him out of the corner of her eye. 'I saw a wedding photograph in the room. Her surname was Blackthorne—I figured it out.'

'Which room?' queried Nicky, drawing on his cigarette, inhaling the smoke and letting it drift out in a long blue-white stream.

Elizabeth told him about the room in the West Wing, about the first time she had heard about it when she had listened at the door to Mark and Abigail's argument. All about the little silver key which fitted the silver lock on the last door in the West Wing, and the fabulously preserved graveyard bedroom of Katherine Fairhaven-Blackthorne.

Nicky listened with growing horror and fascination, his eyes riveted on her. When she had finished he let out a long sigh and shook his head. Elizabeth waited for him to speak, looking at him through her damp lashes.

'If I hadn't met the guy for myself,' Nicky said slowly, 'I'd say he was a dangerous lunatic.'

Elizabeth looked away.

Nicky studied her. 'How did she die, this Katherine Fairhaven-Blackthorne?' He looked at her intently. 'Any idea?'

Elizabeth shrugged. 'No,' she said in a low voice, 'I didn't wait long enough to find out.' Picking at loose threads on the sofa, she blinked back more tears, her vision blurring. 'He tried to make me listen, but I just couldn't stay in that house for another second.'

Nicky watched her shrewdly. 'Because it was her house?' he asked, his eyes gentle.

She nodded. She had felt like a stranger, an intruder. She had felt dirty, cheapened—as though Katherine had been laughing at her with her pretty red mouth and cat-like eyes. It was absurd, but she couldn't reason with her emotions; no one can.

Nicky was still watching her. 'Do you still love him?'

Her eyes stung. 'Of course I do!' she said rawly. You can't turn off that sort of emotion overnight, whatever the provocation. Bending her head, she blinked hard, trying to banish the tears.

Nicky dropped a kiss on her head, stroking her hair comfortingly in silence for a few moments. 'Don't cry,' he said softly. 'We'll sort something out.'

'How?' she asked, her mouth trembling.

Nicky slid a hand under her chin and tilted her head up. 'Look, I've seen Blackthorne with you too many times. I'd swear he felt something more for you than just physical attraction.'

Elizabeth gave him a hurt smile and looked

away. 'I'd like to believe that,' she muttered under her breath.

'I may not be much,' Nicky drawled lightly, 'but I am a man, if nothing else! And I know what a man in love looks like. I'd bet ten to one he's in love with you. The problem is—does he realise it himself?'

Elizabeth frowned. 'I don't understand . . .'

Nicky stubbed out his cigarette. 'Listen—these are the facts. Abigail mentioned a whole load of others; which indicates to me that you're the last in a long line of Katherine F. Blackthorne look-alikes. But——' he raised one long finger, 'he married *you*.'

Elizabeth bit her lip. That was all very well, but Nicky hadn't seen that bedroom, that graveyard. The portrait and the wedding photo-graph, the perfectly preserved beauty of the room.

'Now,' Nicky was saying, 'what you must do is assert your individuality. Go over the top—really spell it out. Make sure he sees Elizabeth Wyatt—not a replica of Katherine.'

Elizabeth glanced at him uncertainly. 'You sound very sure that I'll see him again,' she pointed out in a low voice.

He nodded. 'A hundred per cent,' he said quietly. Lighting another cigarette, he gave her a little smile. 'Trust me, Liz. However tough he seems to be, he's human too.' Grinning, he added, 'I hope!'

Elizabeth sighed, unsure. It was too much to hope for. And even then, how could she ever go back to him? Whatever he might say to her, however good his excuses and explanations, she could never really trust him again, not after this.

It would leap between them like a wall of thorns every time they argued with each other. The strain would break their marriage eventually; whether it was to be broken now or later, the break would come. Elizabeth knew she would suspect him continually, every time he did or said something to upset or worry her, her mind would automatically be turned back towards the mirror, towards the face that represented another woman so cruelly taken from him.

Going upstairs to bed a little while later, Elizabeth got undressed and sat on the edge of her bed in her nightgown, staring at nothing. She was too upset to sleep, too confused to read, and too hurt to think properly.

The face in her mirror stared back at her as though it knew something she didn't. Katherine's face, Elizabeth's face—what difference does it make? she thought. It's what lies behind the features, behind the empty shell, that matters.

Strangely, she found herself dissociating herself from her own face. Trying to look at it long enough for it to become nothing but a shell, an outer covering, while she herself lay inside, trapped behind features which only now were betraying her, destroying her life and happiness.

It isn't me, she thought angrily, and the violet eyes in the mirror simply stared back at her with the same force of hatred. It's only skin and bone. Like a car that has no life unless someone is behind the wheel, driving it, and the way it moves, the speed, the direction, everything about it is governed by the personality of its driver.

Turning away from the mirror, she looked down at her hands. They too were meaningless. Hands were tools, nothing more. Some people used them to grow colourful healthy flowers, others used them to type, answer telephones in offices, build electrical appliances—she used her hands to write songs, play the piano. They were implements, used in a way which best suited their owner.

She raised her face to the mirror again. Cursed with black hair, violet eyes, white, white skin and ruby lips—cursed with a face that haunted the man she loved. How could he ever see her as she was? How could he ever look at her without thinking of Katherine? Two large tears slipped out from beneath her lashes and rolled over those cursed white cheekbones, down to her red mouth.

'I hate you . . .' she whispered, and picked up a china doll, her heart thumping. She hurled it at the mirror. It smashed into a dozen glittering pieces, flying across the room in splinters.

Her shoulders slumped. What difference had that made? Her eye fell on a shard of glass at her feet. The wide violet eyes fringed with black lashes stared at her in the triangular shard of glass.

Elizabeth's hands flew to her face as the tears came again, and she sat sobbing heart-wrenching tears in silence.

CHAPTER EIGHT

DAWN broke over Essex like a freshly cracked egg; yellow-orange light streaking across the sky, running into patches of grey cloud left over from yesterday's storm. Elizabeth woke up and for a moment wondered where she was. Lying across the bed curled up in a little ball, she was freezing. Obviously she had fallen asleep without getting into bed, exhausted by the tears of last night. Looking over at the bare dressing table of her bedroom, she saw the single triangular splinter of glass still left in the mirror. The rest of it lay on the floor. She sighed as she got out of bed and put on slippers and a dressing gown. She didn't want anyone else to see what she had done.

Quickly she picked up the shattered mirror and put it in the wastepaper bin. The last shard was jagged, and as she picked it up, it sliced into her finger, making her gasp as scarlet blood oozed from her fingertip. Frowning, she sucked at the blood, then froze, remembering that night so long ago, when Mark had handed her the white rose, sucked the blood from her wound and kissed her passionately.

Her lower lip trembled. Stop thinking about him! she told herself angrily, and quickly got back into bed, where she lay on her side, trying to empty her mind. It was useless—her mind would not leave his memory.

Getting out of bed, she went over to her chair and got the portable stereo cassette player. She knew exactly what she wanted to hear. She hunted for the cassette and put it on, winding it to the song she was looking for. 'The Day Before You Came' started to flow out from the speakers, and Elizabeth lay back in bed, feeling silent tears start to come, pushing out from under her lashes and sliding wetly over her cheeks.

The girl who had wanted nothing more than to sing, write songs and work with her friends was gone for ever. Her casual, gentle approach to life had disappeared. Suddenly the world seemed a far more painful and disillusioning place. She remembered thinking, only a few days before she met Mark, how good life was, how much there was to do and to be. Now she just felt empty and crushed.

Nicky opened her door at ten o'clock. 'How do you feel?' he asked, watching her from the doorway.

She looked at him with glassy, tear-stained eyes. 'Miserable.'

'Good,' he said briskly, and grinned as she stared at him in amazement, then added, 'Just the right mood to write a really cracking song. I want you downstairs and at the piano in ten minutes' time.'

Elizabeth laughed. 'Tyrant!'

'That's me,' he agreed, adjusting the cuffs of his denim jacket, and went out, closing the door behind him.

Elizabeth got out of bed, her bones aching the way they always do after too much emotional exhaustion and not enough sleep. She creaked over to the door and to the bathroom, showering, and dressing in pale denim jeans and a crisp white shirt.

Nicky was in the kitchen when she arrived downstairs, his dark freshly washed head bent as he read the thin pink pages of the *Financial Times*. He looked up as she came in and went to get herself some coffee.

'Like the outfit,' he said, casting an eye over her pale jeans and white shirt. 'Make sure Mark sees you in that.'

She looked down at herself. 'I look like a miner, forty-niner!'

'Wrong.' Nicky put the paper down. 'You look like Elizabeth Wyatt. I bet K. F. Blackthorne didn't wear jeans the way you do—and I bet she didn't write songs, either.'

Pouring herself some coffee, Elizabeth had to agree that he was right. One tended to try to dress up one's real identity when one was in love; in exactly the same way we turn an ordinary evergreen into a Christmas tree, simply because we feel it ought to be more special. Nicky wanted her to present herself to Mark as she really was, with no coats of veneer.

Nicky watched her with thoughtful eyes. 'Take that coffee into the music room. Start putting those thoughts down on paper—don't waste them.'

She made a face, muttering, 'Taskmaster!' under her breath, but did as she was told, going into the music room and sitting down at the dark brown piano. She stared at the keys as though they might bite her, and slumped on them a moment later, making a dreadful discordant noise issue from the piano.

She smiled sadly. That was exactly how she felt—discordant, wailing. She bashed her hands on the keys again and again until the piano screamed in loud protest.

Nicky put his head round the door. 'What in God's name was that?' he demanded, laughing. '"Winter in Leningrad"?'

Elizabeth laughed too, her eyes sad. 'Absolutely.' A friend of theirs had composed a 'song' entitled 'Winter in Leningrad' when he had lost his girl-friend. It consisted of loud key bashing and howls of anguish. It was a Mayfield classic, brought out as a party piece now and then.

Nicky left the room and she gradually settled down to work. The lyrics wouldn't come at first—her thoughts were too jumbled. But as her fingers slipped over the keys, music started to fit together, a lilting melody appearing in her mind, and she suddenly found a phrase leaping at her out of thin air.

Scribbling it down, she looked at it for a moment. More lyrics came, one after the other, tumbling out of her at a rate of knots while she scribbled them all down, breathing deeply. She stopped, studying what she had written.

'Looking-glass lady with ebony hair,
Tell me what you see when I turn out the light . . .'

She frowned, wondering why the lyric was about Katherine, not Mark, wondering why her mind had instantly turned to the woman in the portrait, his dead wife. But she continued with it, writing well into the late morning, trying to write the music neatly on the slim black stave lines of the manuscript paper in front of her. Nicky only complained if she handed him a sheet of blotchy paper.

By lunchtime, her back was aching from sitting hunched up over the piano. The song was finished, and she was pleased as well as intrigued by it. Only a few loose ends to tidy up lyrically, but it was well structured and had come together quite quickly.

Someone knocked on the door at one o'clock.

It was Ned, a guitarist who had come down for the day. 'Umm,' he said in his strangely absentminded voice, 'we're off to the chippy. Do you want any fish and chips?'

Elizabeth yawned and stretched. 'Please.'

He scratched his head, frowning. 'Umm,' he studied the notepad in his hand, a silver earring dangling from his lobe, 'well, what exactly did you have in mind?' he asked.

Elizabeth smiled. 'Just fish and chips.' It was all too much for Ned, she realised, going past him as he repeated her order under his breath like a little boy, frowning with concentration as he wrote it down.

Going into the living room, she saw Nicky and Jeremy looking out of the window, whispering to each other while everyone else sat round watching them with interest.

'What are you up to?' asked Elizabeth as she went in.

Nicky's head turned. 'Blackthorne's here—just pulled up in an enormous limousine.'

Elizabeth's heart hit her chest painfully and her face fell. 'Oh!' she whispered, feeling her knees go weak.

Nicky was at her side instantly. 'Don't fret,' he guided her to a chair and sat her down. 'Leave it to me—I'll handle it. Don't interrupt anything I say to him.'

She looked at him, alarmed. 'Such as?'

Nicky patted her hand. 'Just leave it to me.'

Elizabeth watched, her pulses leaping fran-

cally, as he went into the hall just as the
oorbell rang sharply through the house. Minutes
eemed to pass with deathly slowness, and no one
nswered the door. Her palms were beginning to
ampen, and she was aware of hot colour
uffusing her cheeks as she met the curious stares
f her friends.

Nicky answered the door on the third sharp
ing. There was a short silence.

Then Mark's voice. 'Is she here?'

'She doesn't want to see you,' Nicky told him
oolly. 'And I can't say I blame her one little bit.
Can you?'

Mark drew a harsh breath. 'She told you,' he
aid deeply, and there was a short pause, then he
aid again, 'But I want to see her. Is she here?'

'Maybe.' Nicky was being deliberately irritat-
ng.

'Don't push your luck, Henderson,' Mark said
rimly. 'I know she's here—the car's outside.
Where else could she be?'

Nicky was silent for a moment, then said, 'Wait
ere. I'll ask if she'll see you.' The door
lammed, and Elizabeth's eyes widened as she
ealised he had slammed it in Mark's face.

Jeremy got up quickly, peering through the old
lue curtains at the doorway. 'He's absolutely
opping mad!' he reported delightedly. 'Steam's
oming out of his ears!'

Nicky came hurrying into the room and took
er arm, standing her up and guiding her back
nto the music room while she just looked at him
a total bewilderment.

'Start playing the song you wrote this
norning,' he said as he seated her at the piano.
Don't stop playing until he's in the room.'

Elizabeth sighed as he closed the music roo door and went back into the hall. Then she flexe her fingers and ran them over the keys, startir to play the song, just as he had told her t Closing her eyes, she sang in high clear tone controlling her voice so that it danced in ric notes against the lilting music from the pian The door opened, and she faltered, her hea thumping madly, but she didn't open her eye even when the door closed again. Mark was in tl room, she felt his presence, but she continued sing, until she had finished the song, then she s back, pulses leaping in silence.

Opening her eyes again, she looked over at tl doorway. Mark was watching her with those dee blue eyes. 'You're very talented,' he said quietl

Elizabeth looked away, her heart hurting. ' talent you wanted to stop,' she said, and w angry with herself because there was too muc raw emotion in her voice.

Mark watched her intently. 'I didn't want lose you,' he said deeply. 'A career like th would come between us.'

'Between us?' she queried, her voice cold. 'B there is nothing between us any more. You mac sure of that, Mark.'

He drew a shaky breath. 'I wouldn't stop yc now, I promise.'

Elizabeth closed the piano lid carefully, n willing to have an emotional argument with him this time. She wasn't enough in control yet, sl knew she would just burst into tears if they argue too passionately, and that would weaken he would cause her too much pain and anguish.

'Well,' she said slowly, not looking at hin 'that's neither here nor there now.'

Mark studied her, his eyes intent. 'Because of Katherine?'

She nodded silently. There were a thousand questions buzzing around in her mind, questions she desperately wanted him to answer. But she couldn't bring herself to ask him, couldn't quite summon up the iron control she needed to stay calm, when what she really wanted to do was scream at him and hit him for hurting her so badly.

He was watching her fixedly. 'Katherine died three years ago. It's true—I found it difficult to forget her at first——'

'Difficult?' she said bitterly. 'You were obsessed with her! You kept a shrine to her in your house, for God's sake!'

Mark drew a harsh breath. 'It just happened—I didn't plan it. When she died I couldn't bring myself to throw her things out, so I kept them, and Mrs Bayliss looked after the room.' He searched her face, his eyes intense. 'But I'd forgotten it existed.'

'Liar!' she snapped, her eyes hating him. 'I heard you and Abigail, that night in the storm. I was outside the door.'

He was silent for a moment, taken aback, staring at her. She wondered why it hadn't occurred to him before now that she had been aware of some kind of secret in the house—she had mentioned it to him often enough, trying to make him tell her. But he had probably assumed she was just playing on instinct instead of facts.

'I see,' he said deeply, and she threw him an angry smile, saying:

'Yes. You see.'

Mark stood for a moment in silence, then knelt

by her chair to look up at her. 'I married yo
because I loved you, Elizabeth—not because yo
look like my dead wife.'

'Really.' Elizabeth looked away, her voice flat.

'At first it was because you looked like her,
admit that. But after the first week or so, I foun
myself falling in love with you. By the time
asked you to marry me, I'd completely forgotte
Katherine.'

Elizabeth's heart hurt. She couldn't believ
him. Suddenly she stood up, pushing away th
piano stool and going over to the door to open it
refusing to listen to him any longer.

'Goodbye, Mark.' She held the door ope
tears stinging her eyes, although she blinked har
to make them go away. It was too painful to liste
to him for another second.

Mark stood up slowly. 'You can't mean it,' h
said deeply.

'I do!' How could she ever believe him? It wa
pointless discussing it with him. However muc
she wanted to believe that he really loved he
there would always be that doubt, that naggin
fear that he didn't see her at all, just her face.

He studied her intensely for a long momen
Then: 'I can't make you stay with me. But I'
like to ask a favour from you, before you make u
your mind for good.'

'It's already made up,' she said, her thro
burning with a need to cry.

Mark slid his hands in his pockets, looking at th
floor. 'My grandmother arrived at Carthax toda
and she wants to meet you.' He shrugged. 'I can
bring myself to tell her you've left me. I'd be ve
grateful if you'd come to the house. Just meet he
pretend everything's all right between us.'

Elizabeth shook her head. 'It's impossible.'

He looked at her, his heart in his eyes. 'Please,' he said deeply. 'It would break her heart if she didn't meet you. She's nearly eighty-five and I very rarely see her. Just meet her, this once, let her think I've found someone who'll give her great-grandchildren.'

Elizabeth looked at him angrily, resenting him for putting her in this position. How could she refuse to do it? He was putting the responsibility of an old woman's happiness on her shoulders. She looked at him, her face cold.

'Surely she'll spot the resemblance?' she said angrily. 'Do you really think it'll make her happy to see you've married a replica of Katherine?'

Mark blinked, black lashes flickering on his tanned cheeks. 'That's a risk I'll have to take. She's always been very fond of me. She wants to be sure I'm happy.'

Elizabeth sighed deeply. It was a cleft stick. What on earth was she supposed to say to that? She shoved her hands into the pockets of her denim jeans, frowning as she stared at the floor. She would have to go, there wasn't really much choice. She could hurt Mark, even though it was hurting her, but she couldn't bring herself to hurt an innocent old lady, shatter her illusions.

'I suppose you want me to go now?' she said resentfully.

'Please.' Mark was watching her intently.

She lifted her head with defiant anger. 'And I suppose you also want me to change before we go?'

His eyes softened. 'Not at all,' he said huskily. 'I think you look beautiful. You should wear jeans more often.'

She stared in surprise, then frowned, perplexed

and nodded. 'I'll get my coat,' she said slowly and walked into the hall to pick up her sheepskin coat which was hung casually over the newel post of the grimy white-painted staircase. That remark didn't add up to what she had thought of him previously. From the look of Katherine's wardrobes, she would have died before wearing jeans. Her wardrobes had been stacked full of silk, satin and furs—not a casual outfit in sight.

'Liz?' Nicky appeared in the hall as she was shouldering into her coat while Mark held it for her, standing behind her. He frowned as he saw them together and asked, 'Is everything okay?'

'We're just going for a drive,' Mark told him coolly, and opened the front door, standing in the doorway waiting for Elizabeth as she followed him reluctantly.

Nicky prevaricated. 'Oh . . .' He watched them unsure of whether or not to interfere.

'She'll be quite safe with me,' Mark said quietly. 'You don't need to worry.'

Nicky looked at him for a moment, then nodded, and they went outside, closing the front door behind them. Crane wasn't driving today, so Mark opened the front door of the limousine and helped her in before going round to the driver's seat. Elizabeth watched him in silence as he swung the enormous car away from Mayfield, driving along the narrow lanes to Carthax.

They didn't speak as they drove to Carthax. Elizabeth looked out of the window, a dozen questions buzzing through her mind, but she said not a word. The atmosphere was, strangely, not as tense as she had thought it would be, and she wondered why.

*   *   *

'I told her you were visiting friends,' said Mark as he went into Carthax House through the double oak doors. 'She's waiting in the drawing room.'

Elizabeth nodded and followed him in while the butler closed the doors behind them and disappeared, as faceless as always. They went silently down the long red-carpeted corridor towards the drawing room, and Elizabeth swallowed tightly, afraid of what Mark's grandmother would say when she saw her.

Mark opened the door quietly. A fire was burning in the grate, the room warm and cheerful as the big shiny Christmas tree reflected prettily in the gilt mirror over the fireplace.

'Mark?' A frail old voice came from behind the chair by the fire. 'Is that you?'

Mark closed the door. 'Yes, Nanna.' He looked across at the big winged leather chair the old lady sat in, its back to them. 'I've brought Elizabeth home.'

One bony arm with loose mottled skin waved from behind the winged chair. 'Come here, my dear,' she said in a reedlike voice. 'I've been looking forward to meeting you.'

Elizabeth glanced at Mark worriedly. He nodded, giving her a gentle push forwards, and she went slowly over to the fire.

Old Mrs Blackthorne was tiny, her thin body covered by a thick blanket over her knees. The black dress she wore with a simple string of pearls had a high collar, but not high enough to hide the loose folds of skin at her neck.

'My dear, you must forgive me,' she said softly, her hair like soft white drifts of candy-

floss on her head, 'but my doctor advised me no
to attend your wedding. The excitement, you
see—it would have been too much for me.'

Elizabeth smiled. 'That's all right,' she said
gently, and frowned as she suddenly noticed the
way the old lady stared at her, blankly, looking a
a point just past her shoulder.

The watery blue eyes stared at nothing, sunken
into hollowed fragile sockets. 'I'm so glad Mark ha
found someone at last,' she said softly, and her pale
pink lips moved in a smile. 'He's been unhappy fo
a long time. Won't you sit down, my dear?'

Elizabeth watched in slowly dawning realisation
as the old lady leaned over blindly, the thin
arthritic fingers groping for the arm of the chair
beside her, finding and tapping it, her head still
turned to Elizabeth with unseeing eyes.

She's blind, Elizabeth thought with sudden
clarity, and felt herself sink slowly into the chair
still staring in astonishment. The old woman
leaned back with a sigh, her skull visible through
the thin layer of skin at her hairline.

'Mark?' she said in her high fragile voice. 'Why
don't you organise some tea for us?'

Mark came forward and dropped a kiss on her
sunken cheek. 'Anything you say, Nanna,' he said
quietly, and turned, going out of the room
leaving them alone together in front of the fire.

'Mark tells me you sing like a nightingale,' old
Mrs Blackthorne said as the door closed. 'He'
very proud of you.'

Elizabeth stared, amazed. 'Did he say that?'

The old lady chuckled. 'He didn't need to!
She patted Elizabeth's hand blindly. 'I can tell. I
hope you'll sing for me one day. There's a piano
in the house—did you know that?'

'Yes,' Elizabeth smiled, 'I've been using it. And I'd love to sing for you.'

The old lady sighed deeply, smiling. 'I'm so glad. It's years since there was music in this house. I bought the piano for my late husband— he was a wonderful pianist. But the music died with him, I'm afraid.'

Elizabeth smiled. 'It's still in tune. Someone must be looking after it.'

Mrs Blackthorne nodded her white head. 'That'll be Mrs Bayliss, I expect.'

There was a short pause in conversation, and Elizabeth took the opportunity to study her with curious eyes. She must have been very beautiful when she was young; the high cheekbones and delicately chiselled nose were still evident in her old age, and the watery blue eyes which stared so emptily held a spark of lost vitality in their depths. Elizabeth wondered how she had lost her sight. There were no visible scars, so it couldn't have been in an accident.

'I've been so worried about Mark,' Mrs Blackthorne said into the silence. 'Ever since Katherine died, it's as if he's been locked up inside himself. Her death seemed to snuff out the vitality in him.' She paused, frowning. 'I presume he told you about her?'

Elizabeth's throat tightened. 'Yes.'

The old lady nodded. 'Poor Katherine! She was such a silly child. She begged Mark to buy her that wretched horse.' She sighed. 'But that's all in the past. Tell me about yourself, Elizabeth. I want to know everything about you.'

Elizabeth hesitated, wondering what she had meant about the horse. Had she been talking about Sultan? she wondered. Slowly, she began to tell Mrs Blackthorne about herself, her family and her work. As she talked about her singing, her songwriting and her ambitions, she forgot her unhappiness about Mark, and noticed that Mrs Blackthorne was listening with genuine interest, her pale smile seemingly at odds with the dead, lifeless eyes. It was strange to watch someone whose animated smile was accompanied by expressionless, half-closed eyes.

'You lost your parents, too?' Mrs Blackthorne enquired as Elizabeth told her about the accident.

'Two years ago,' said Elizabeth, nodding, then realised how silly that was; how could Mrs Blackthorne see she was nodding?

'You sound sad,' the old lady frowned, her lids half-closed. 'Do you miss them very much?'

'I did,' Elizabeth admitted, and smiled. 'But Mark seems to have stopped that to a large extent. As though he's taken their place.'

Mrs Blackthorne nodded her wispy white head. 'I quite understand, my dear. I felt the same when I met his grandfather.' She smiled fondly. 'He was a wonderful man—very similar to Mark in many respects.'

Elizabeth smiled at the tone of fond remembrance in the old woman's gently lined face. 'If he was anything like Mark, I'm sure I would have fallen for him too.'

Mrs Blackthorne smiled. 'You're quite right, my dear. Edward was absolutely irresistible—charm simply oozed from his fingertips. I was the envy of all London and Essex in my day——' she smiled. 'He was quite a catch, you know.'

Elizabeth laughed, trying to picture Edward Blackthorne. She came up with an image of Mark dressed in Edwardian or Victorian clothes, and possibly a trim black moustache. It made her smile, forgetting for a moment her anger with him.

Mrs Blackthorne said suddenly, 'I'm so glad we've met at last. Mark's been a different man since he found you. You've blown all the cobwebs out of this old house, laid Katherine's ghost to rest. I was very worried about Mark. He seemed so . . .' she frowned, her fingers groping as she searched for a word to describe him, 'so lost. After Katherine, I mean.'

Elizabeth looked at her uncertainly, but said nothing. How could she believe that, much as she wanted to? But she didn't want to upset the old lady's illusions.

'I wish I could see what you look like,' Mrs Blackthorne sighed. 'Would you mind very much if I felt your face? It's the only way I can get a clear picture of you, you see.'

Elizabeth's pulses leapt. 'Felt my face?' she repeated, not knowing quite what to do. The old lady must have felt Katherine's face too; she would know immediately.

The old woman smiled. 'I know it sounds strange, but my fingers can tell me what my eyes can't. If you just kneel down here in front of me, let me touch your face.'

Elizabeth swallowed, her heart leaping. Slowly she got out of her chair and knelt down in front of the old woman. She looked towards the door. Where on earth was Mark?

'That's it.' Mrs Blackthorne leaned forward, fingers groping blindly for Elizabeth's face. They touched her forehead and she sighed, but Elizabeth went icy cold as the thin fingertips ran slowly over her features, tracing her eyes, nose, mouth and cheeks. 'What colour is your hair?' she asked, frowning with concentration.

'Black,' Elizabeth said huskily, and the frail hands moved to her hair at the side.

'It's so thick and curly!' she exclaimed. 'It's natural, isn't it? You don't use electric things to help it along?'

Elizabeth couldn't help laughing. 'No,' she agreed, 'it's natural.'

'And your eyes—what colour are they?'

Elizabeth swallowed. 'Blue.'

Mrs Blackthorne sighed contentedly. 'Blue,' she murmured with a smile, 'the same colouring as Mark. You must make a beautiful couple.'

Mrs Blackthorne let her hands slip from Elizabeth's face, and Elizabeth almost sighed with relief, although she was perplexed that the old lady hadn't noticed the resemblance to Katherine.

'My dear,' Mrs Blackthorne took Elizabeth's hands after searching for them, 'I'm so glad Mark found you. You're so different from Katherine.'

Elizabeth stared, shocked.

The old lady was smiling, saying, 'I was very worried because he kept saying he wanted to find someone just like her. But he found you, didn't he, and you're nothing like her.'

After a moment's incredulous silence, Elizabeth felt her hands tighten on the old lady's, clutching the thin fingers in her own as if for reassurance.

'What was she like?' she asked huskily.

'Katherine?' Mrs Blackthorne smiled, brows raised. 'She had a sharp voice and very restless movements. Like a little girl, really, in many ways. Always talking about herself and begging Mark to buy her pretty things.'

Carefully, Elizabeth said, 'But she was very beautiful, wasn't she?'

The old lady smiled. 'No, my dear, I don't think she was,' she said softly, and paused for a moment, listening to the silence in the room, the spitting fire in the grate. Then she pressed Elizabeth's hands and said, 'You're far more beautiful. You're gentle and kind, where she was spoilt and self-indulgent. Some people are just not built for giving, and Katherine, rest her poor soul, was one of them.' She leaned forward, smiling. 'Your whole life is built on giving. That's what art is—and that's what love is.'

Elizabeth's lower lip trembled. 'Thank you,' she said huskily, and the old woman patted her hand.

'That's quite all right, my dear,' she said gently, and Elizabeth stood up, going back to sit down on her own chair.

The door opened at that moment, and Mark came in with the tea. He looked at Elizabeth anxiously, and she avoided his eyes, truth beginning to dawn on her.

'Have you been talking about me, Nanna?' he asked lightly, pouring his grandmother a cup of tea and bringing it over to her. He took her thin hand and guided it to the cup, putting it gently in her fingers.

'Of course,' she agreed, smiling as she groped for the handle of the cup blindly, taking it with great care not to spill any. 'What else? And a very interesting chat we had, too. Didn't we, my dear?'

Elizabeth looked at Mark, her eyes clear. 'Very interesting,' she agreed softly. Mrs Blackthorne thought she was just teasing her grandson, but

Elizabeth was deadly serious as she looked at Mark.

Mark studied her open face for a long moment, then he bent his dark head to kiss his grandmother. 'You're a wicked old lady!' he told her affectionately.

Elizabeth watched as he handed his grandmother a biscuit, helping her to take it, and watching carefully to see that she didn't spill any of the scalding tea on herself by accident. She was amazed at his obvious concern for the old woman, the gentleness with which he treated her. But he had been gentle towards her too, in the past, she now realised. Only she had been so busy worrying about the secret in the West Wing that she hadn't noticed it before.

They talked by the fire for another hour, their conversation lazy and relaxed. Mark and his grandmother obviously had a very close relationship, Elizabeth observed, and she wondered why he had never mentioned her before now, why she had never met the white-haired old lady before. Mark was obviously deeply fond of her; his careful, watchful gaze didn't leave her for a moment.

Mark walked his grandmother to the car while Crane waited silently in chauffeur's uniform beside the limousine. The old lady held on to Mark's arm, tapping her silver-topped ebony cane on the ground in front of her with slow careful movements.

'Oh, how lovely!' Mrs Blackthorne exclaimed as she stepped into the grounds in front of the house. 'I can smell spring. And I can feel the sun again.' The lifeless blue-white eyes stared unseeingly up at the sky. She rattled Mark's arm, smiling. 'Be my eyes, Mark. Tell me what it looks like.'

Mark looked down at her fondly. 'Do you remember the Christmas Abigail was born? You and Grandfather took me for a treasure hunt in the grounds, on Christmas Day when the sun came out.'

Mrs Blackthorne nodded happily, sighing. 'Yes, I remember. We hid the treasure in a tree, and you climbed it just like a little monkey.' She laughed. 'Then Edward had to help you down because you were stuck!'

Mark laughed too. 'Well, that's what it looks like.'

The old lady nodded slowly. 'Yes, I can smell it—clean and fresh and new. I love January, don't you?'

Elizabeth stood a few steps behind, watching them, two generations apart, but meeting in the middle as Mark held the frail white-haired lady, his dark head bent towards hers, his body lean with youth and strength.

Elizabeth stood with Mark's arm round her as they waved Mrs Blackthorne away, watching until the long black limousine had disappeared down the long drive and off the estate.

Mark turned to look at her. 'Thank you,' he said deeply.

Elizabeth studied him. 'Why didn't you tell me she was blind?'

'Can't you guess?'

Elizabeth eyed him steadily for a moment, then nodded. She could guess all right. He had wanted her to be exposed to the sensitivity of blindness. Mrs Blackthorne's approach to life was through the senses she had left, each sharpened by her lack of sight. And with it came a simplistic view which made Elizabeth's fear and anger dissipate immediately, showing her that although she shared the same face as Katherine Fairhaven-Blackthorne, the similarity ended there. To a blind old lady, she was a totally different person from Mark's first wife. It not only gave her her sense of identity back, it also mellowed her anger towards Mark.

He was watching her intently. 'Do you want me to drive you home now?'

Elizabeth shook her head. 'I want you to tell me about Katherine.'

CHAPTER NINE

'SULTAN threw her,' said Mark, sitting opposite her in the elegant drawing room. 'She was dead before I could reach her. Her neck snapped like a wishbone on impact.'

Elizabeth watched him with saddened eyes. 'How awful,' she said quietly, trying to imagine the horror of it as she pictured it—Mark running to his wife, only to find she was dead. 'No wonder you were so angry when you saw me riding him!'

Mark shot her a grim smile. 'Angry, but not frightened. It wasn't Sultan's fault, you see—he's actually a good horse. I'm afraid Katherine ill-treated him appallingly.'

'But you sold him,' she pointed out with a frown, 'immediately after I'd ridden him.'

He inclined his dark head. 'I didn't want anything in this house to remind me of her. Once I married you—before I married you—I wanted to make it your house, not hers.'

'But the bedroom . . .' she began.

'Will be empty by the end of January,' he cut in, watching her. 'I called Sothebys in weeks ago. They valued everything—it's all antique, you see. They've got an auction coming up in February that it's perfect for.' He studied her closely. 'It was just unfortunate that you saw it before they'd taken everything away.'

Elizabeth nodded slowly, understanding at once. Of course, she had found out when he least expected her to, and she wondered why he had allowed it to happen so easily.

'You must have wanted me to find out, though,' she said, voicing her thoughts. 'You gave me the keys, after all.'

'Purely unconscious, I assure you,' he said with a dry smile. 'It didn't occur to me that you'd use them so soon. I was going to take the silver key off the ring the next day. But I was obviously too late.'

She studied him for a long moment, then said quietly, 'Would you have told me, Mark? Eventually?'

He sighed deeply, running long fingers over his brow. 'I think so. But it was very difficult. Every now and then, I'd make up my mind to break it to you gently.' He reddened, the tanned flesh colouring slightly. 'But I lost my nerve every time!'

Elizabeth thought back over the past two or three months that she had known him, and was able to pinpoint moments when he had seemed to be about to tell her, but had drawn back at the last minute. They were vague memories, and at the time she had paid no attention to them. But now, as she looked back with open eyes, she could see that what he said was true. He had intended to tell her. But she could see now that the secret in the West Wing had been one which needed careful handling. What would she have thought if he had told her? If he had taken her upstairs to that beautiful shrine to show her that her face had once belonged to another woman? A woman he had so obviously worshipped.

Looking at him, she asked quietly, 'Did you love her very much?'

Mark studied her intently. 'Yes, I did.'

Elizabeth looked away, turning her head. What had she expected him to say?

Mark reached out and took her chin with gentle fingers, turning her face back to look at him. 'How could I help loving her?' he asked softly. 'She was so young and beautiful, so full of life. She was a child-woman—anything could make her happy—a puppy, a rainbow, a new dress.'

'She sounds very nice,' Elizabeth said bitterly.

He laughed, shaking his head. 'She lost interest in five seconds flat. It didn't matter what I bought her—it was discarded almost immediately. She didn't even care if it was alive—puppies and new clothes were all the same to her. She just ignored them once they were hers.'

Elizabeth frowned. Katherine sounded like a spoilt child, and that was exactly the way Mrs Blackthorne had described her—only the old lady had sensed something else in Mark's dead wife— a sharpness, she had said, a complete obsession with herself.

Mark watched her with gentle eyes. 'I loved her the way one loves a pretty butterfly dancing in the sunshine. But I didn't know her. I couldn't share anything with her. I couldn't talk to her.' He smiled, shaking his head. 'I could only watch her.'

'You still loved her,' Elizabeth said jealously, and frowned at herself. How absurd to be jealous of the dead!

Mark smiled. 'Not the way I love you,' he said simply.

She flushed deeply, wanting to believe it badly. 'Explain!' she said huskily.

He frowned. 'How can I? You can't put feelings like that into words—except to say that when I feel lonely, I think of you, want to be with you. When I'm happy, I want to rush home and share it with you, tell you about it. When there's a problem I want to turn to you.'

Elizabeth waited, wanting more. She could understand what he was saying, but her insecurity about him had grown to monstrous proportions after discovering the shrine to Katherine, seeing her face.

Mark studied her, black lashes flickering against his tanned cheek. Then he laughed softly. 'All right, let me put it another way. Someone once said—"To love is nothing, to be loved is something, but to love and be loved is everything."' He stopped, watching her. 'Does that explain it to you?'

Elizabeth bit her lip, looking at him through her lashes. 'Katherine didn't love you, but you loved her?' she suggested, and he laughed, shaking his head.

'Why do I get the feeling you're going to haul me over the coals?' he enquired, his eyes alight with amusement.

Her brows rose. 'Because you deserve to be.'

Mark sobered immediately. 'Elizabeth, I can only tell you that I want to be with you, always. I think of you always. I get a high just from talking to you. You give me confidence when I need it, you calm me when I'm frantic.'

She looked at him, amazed. 'When do I?' she exclaimed. 'I've never noticed you frantic or uncertain.'

He laughed. 'You're kidding! Did you think I wasn't human?'

'It had occurred to me.'

He studied her, his eyes serious. 'Maybe it doesn't show often enough,' he said quietly, 'but it's there. I'm just as vulnerable as anyone else.'

Elizabeth nodded, meeting his eyes and seeing the sincerity there. He didn't seem distant now—he hadn't ever since she had discovered Katherine's shrine upstairs. Perhaps the weight of secrecy had been what made him draw away from her in the past, become remote. In fact she could see now that he had only ever been cool or offhand with her when she had mentioned something that could have connected in his mind with Katherine.

'So what happens now?' said Mark into the sudden silence. 'Do you stay or go?'

He was watching her intently, and Elizabeth turned her head to meet his gaze frankly. She hadn't decided yet—it was too hard. She knew very well that she wanted to stay, badly. But she also knew she didn't yet have the strength to trust him completely, not after what had happened this time around.

'I need some time to think,' she told him. 'On my own.'

Mark looked away, his black lashes flickering against his tanned cheek. 'Of course,' he said deeply, staring at his long fingertips in apparent fascination.

She looked at him through her lashes. 'Will you drive me back to Mayfield?'

He hesitated, then sighed and stood up. 'Of course,' he said again, and Elizabeth could see that he was very scared that she might not come back. But although she wanted to reassure him, she also knew that Nicky had been right when he had said she must assert her individuality. If she gave in to Mark without a struggle, he would never respect her enough to make a marriage work.

They walked to the car, and Mark dismissed Crane, getting into the driver's seat himself while Elizabeth sat beside him. They pulled away smoothly from the house, Mark's hands strong on the powerful steering wheel as they drove along through the Essex countryside.

'Let me ask you one thing,' said Elizabeth as they sped towards Mayfield. 'Why did you give me the ruby choker? It was hers, wasn't it?'

Mark blinked. 'It was hers,' he agreed slowly.

'I saw it in the painting,' she told him, glancing at him across the plush interior of the limousine. 'Why did you want me to wear it?'

He sighed, looking straight ahead at the road. 'I don't know that you'd consider my motives sound enough.'

She frowned. 'What does that mean?' she asked with an attempt at humour.

Mark flicked her a quick look. 'I had to be absolutely certain that it was you I loved, not Katherine's image,' he said slowly. 'That's why I wanted you in white all the time—to try to make it your colour, not hers.'

Elizabeth stared, feeling deeply disappointed. 'So you weren't certain—even at Christmas?'

'Oh, I was certain, all right,' he told her with a grim smile. 'But the ruby choker was the final hurdle, if you like. Once I saw you wearing it, and knew it was you I was looking at, I knew everything was all right.'

Elizabeth studied him as he drove through the village of Mayfield towards the house. 'Did she wear it a lot?'

Mark nodded. 'All the time.' He laughed. 'It was the only thing she ever really liked.'

They pulled up outside Mayfield. Elizabeth noticed heads peering out of the window, the curtains pulled back a fraction. Yellow light streamed out through the open curtains—it was getting dark now. Soon night would have fallen, and the sky was dusky grey, the few street lamps of the village already switched on.

Mark switched the engine off, and they sat in silence for a while. Then he turned to look at her.

'When will I see you?' he asked deeply.

Elizabeth looked at him and shook her head slowly. 'I don't know, Mark. Soon.'

He flicked off his headlights with one long finger. 'I don't want you to feel pressurised,' he said quietly, 'so I'll make an arrangement with you.'

She nodded, waiting. 'Go on.'

'I'll come here tomorrow, at three o'clock in the afternoon,' he told her. 'If you want to see me—if you want to come back to me—put a single red rose in the window.'

Elizabeth caught her breath, deeply moved by the romanticism in the idea. 'A red rose?'

He nodded. 'I'll see it from here. If it's there, I'll come in and take you home to Carthax. If the window is empty——' he paused, looking away from her, 'I'll never see you again. I'll leave you in peace.'

Elizabeth nodded. Opening the car door, she got out, saying, 'A red rose. Three o'clock.'

Mark waited until she had gone, then the engine flared into life, and he drove away from her, red tail lights flashing as the long black limousine disappeared from sight. Elizabeth watched from the doorway with a little smile. She knew that tomorrow, at three o'clock, there would be a single red rose in the window.

It was at lunchtime that she drove into the village to go to the flower shop. Looking for somewhere to park, she tried to get as close to the flower shop as possible before locking her car and walking across the road to it. The window had a small assortment of carnations, iris and lilies among other things. Her heart sank. Not a rose in sight.

The door rang gently as she opened it, and a few seconds later the assistant came out from behind a beaded curtain at the back of the shop, giving her a bright smile as she did so.

'Good afternoon, miss.' The woman brushed down a neat silver bun with dainty hands. 'What can I do for you?'

'Well,' Elizabeth looked around the shop anxiously, 'I wanted some red roses. You don't appear to have any on display, though.'

The assistant made a face. 'I'm sorry, miss, we're fresh out of them. We have to have them brought over specially.' She gave her a bright smile. 'We have some nice red carnations, though.'

Elizabeth shook her head, worried. 'It has to be roses. Is there another branch nearby that might have some?'

'I don't rightly know, miss,' the woman said, but added helpfully, 'I'll check for you, though, if you'd like to wait here.'

The minutes ticked past agonisingly while Elizabeth waited, wandering around the shop listening to the woman's successive telephone calls to several local branches. Glancing at her watch, she saw it was one-thirty, and Mark would be at Mayfield in an hour and a half. Hurry up! she thought, watching the woman on the telephone.

'You're in luck, miss.' The assistant re-appeared. 'They've got two dozen at St Mark's, ten miles away. Do you know it?'

Elizabeth almost laughed at the coincidence in names. 'I know it,' she said, and thanked the woman before hurrying out of the shop and over to her car. She drove quickly to St Mark's and was lucky not to find much traffic on the roads to slow her down.

The little flower shop was on the main road through St Mark's, and Elizabeth found a parking space right opposite it. She dashed over to the shop and decided to buy the whole two dozen red roses! That would be a surprise for Mark, she thought, smiling as she clutched them in her hand and came out of the shop.

She didn't see the car. It came up over the brow of the hill and didn't have time to stop. Elizabeth was already halfway across the road when she heard someone call out to her.

'Look out!' an elderly gentleman waved his walking stick at her.

She turned just in time to see the car heading for her, bonnet gleaming in the sunlight, and she started to run out of its path. The driver saw her, slammed on the brakes and screeched to a halt— but it was a fraction of a second too late.

The red roses flew out of her hand as the wing of the car smashed into her left leg. White-hot pain shot through her and she caught her breath in lurching agony. The black tarmac came up to thud into her head as she fell, her leg twisting at a sickly angle beneath her.

A crowd gathered, concerned faces zeroed in and out of her hazy vision. 'I didn't see her!' The driver was standing beside her, talking frantically. 'She just stepped out into the road!'

Elizabeth frowned against the pain in her head and peered up, to see the elderly gentleman bending towards her, his little tweed hat perched on his grey head.

'It's all right, miss, just lie still,' the old gentleman said in a cut-glass, frightfully English voice. 'An ambulance is on its way.'

Absurdly disconnected thoughts ran through her head and she nodded, wondering if he was an ex-Army man. Then she remembered Mark, and her eyes opened wide. 'My roses!' she exclaimed on the end of her breath. 'Where are my roses?' And she passed out.

The ambulance juddered to a halt outside the hospital just as Elizabeth woke up. She felt queasy, and disorientated, gazing around her with a dazed expression. A fat orange blanket covered her aching body, and she looked down at herself to see her hands were swollen and puffy, the knuckles throbbing with dull pain.

'Took a nasty tumble there, didn't you?' The ambulanceman was just getting up to open the double doors, and he gave her a kindly smile as he and his colleague began to lift the stretcher out of the vehicle. 'Don't worry, though, you'll be right as rain in no time.'

'My leg hurts,' Elizabeth told them stupidly, aware of shrieking pain every time she tried to flex the muscles in her lower leg. She was scared to move it in case she felt a nauseating scrape of bone against bone, which she knew would make her feel utterly sick.

'I'm not surprised!' The elder of the two ambulancemen said. 'It's a lovely shade of purple.'

Elizabeth stared, aghast. 'Was there much blood?' she asked in a whisper, thinking aloud.

The man laughed, eyes crinkling up. 'Quite the little tragedy queen!' he said cheerfully, and winked. 'No, love, no blood at all. Probably just a broken ankle. They'll have you on the mend in seconds.'

She sank back on the trolley as they wheeled her in. Watching the long rows of strip-lighting pass overhead on the ceiling from her horizontal position, she wondered how long it would take to see to her ankle.

Mark would be at Mayfield in an hour, and there wasn't a single red rose in the window. Elizabeth bit her lip anxiously. Maybe she could get someone to ring him and tell him what had happened. Casualty departments were notoriously slow when it came to minor breakages like hers.

'Road accident for you, Jocelyn!' The ambulanceman wheeled her towards a petite nurse in Casualty. 'Bumped into a car and hurt herself.'

'Don't let Staff hear you talk like that about the patients!' said the nurse with a high-cheekboned smile. 'You know how formal she is.'

The ambulanceman grinned and saluted, then sauntered off whistling. Nurse Jocelyn looked at Elizabeth with a calm smile, and Elizabeth was amazed at the delicacy of her olive-skinned features. The dark eyes that held such depth and kindness were strangely reassuring. Why do nurses always look so serene? Elizabeth wondered.

'How do you feel?' asked the nurse, and Elizabeth made a face.

'Not so good!' She glanced at the round white clock in the corner and frowned. 'I'm supposed to be meeting my husband in an hour. Could you ring him and tell him what's happened? It's terribly important.'

The nurse nodded her dark head. 'Of course, I'll see to it as soon as you're with the doctor.'

Elizabeth relaxed and gave her the telephone number of Carthax House, then lay back and waited until another nurse was summoned to wheel her to the doctor's office. He examined her leg and hands, and pronounced her to have a broken ankle and minor cuts and bruises. Elizabeth waited for what seemed hours while the X-rays were completed and sent back, then she was sent off to be set in plaster and bandaged.

At five o'clock she was finally wheeled back to the exit from Casualty, and her eyes scanned the department for a sign of Mark's black head. But he was nowhere to be seen. Surely he would have come straight to the hospital, she thought worriedly. He would know that if she wanted to get in touch with him about it, she wanted to come back to him. Surely he would realise that! Worry set in, and she looked around for the nurse she had spoke to originally to find out what Mark had said on the telephone.

Nurse Jocelyn, as Elizabeth thought of her, was standing by the window in her crisp white uniform, her dark head bent as she wrote on a series of little white cards.

'Oh, hello,' she said as Elizabeth was wheeled towards her by the orderly. 'Everything fixed?'

Elizabeth pointed to her leg, now in plaster

Just about,' she said with a smile. 'Did you manage to get through to my husband?'

'Oh . . .!' The nurse's hand flew to her mouth in dismay. 'I'm terribly sorry, I forgot all about it! There was an emergency just after you'd left— a suicide. It completely put it out of my mind.'

Elizabeth's heart stopped. Staring at the nurse, she heard herself whisper, 'Oh my God!' Mark didn't know. He hadn't been told. He thought she didn't want him any more. She had to get to a phone. Panic set in and she felt her palms begin to sweat.

'Do you want me to ring him now?' Nurse Jocelyn picked up a telephone with fine-boned fingers, her face apologetic.

'Please.' Elizabeth watched with a strained face as the nurse dialled Mark's number and waited for it to be answered.

Elizabeth whitened as she listened to the conversation. Mark wasn't there—she could gather that from the look on the nurse's face. Where was he, then? she thought, panicking. How would she get in touch with him and let him know it was all right?

The nurse put the receiver down a moment later. 'He wasn't there,' she said quietly, and bit her lip with small white teeth. 'I'm terribly sorry about this—his housekeeper said he'd left hours ago.'

'Left?' Elizabeth tensed, staring. 'For where?'

'America.'

Elizabeth's jaw dropped open. 'America?' she echoed stupidly, and her eyes were wide and pained.

The nurse nodded. 'New York.' Watching her with a frown, she asked, 'Can I get you some water or something? You've gone awfully pale.'

'Water?' Elizabeth hesitated for a moment then shook her head. 'No, thank you. I'd rathe you got me a taxi.'

The nurse picked up the telephone again 'Where to?' she asked as she dialled with a pen.

'Heathrow Airport, Terminal Three, Elizabeth said quickly. Concorde was her onl chance. If Mark was going to New York, h had to be travelling by Concorde, she was sur of it. And she had to get to the airport befor he took off.

'I really am awfully sorry.' Nurse Jocelyn cam over to her when she had rung off. 'It was one o those things—everything falls to the waysid when there's an emergency. And suicides alway depress me so much. I always feel angry.' Sh shook her dark head and folded her arms. 'It' such a waste. We work so hard to save life.'

Elizabeth watched her, realising how small he own problem was. At least she was still alive. A least she could get to Mark, tell him she loved him still. At least he hadn't got a telephone cal telling him she was dead. She shivered, glad tha her leg was in plaster when it could have beer much, much worse.

She looked at the nurse with a sad frown. 'I must be awful for you. Do you ever see anyone you know?'

The nurse looked down, dark lashes sweeping her dusky cheeks. 'I went to school near here Sometimes it's someone I knew at school on the operating table, and she can't even hear me because she's swallowed so many sleeping pills. Her gaze flicked back to Elizabeth's with a wry smile. 'Sorry! I didn't mean to go on. If Matron

eard me she'd put me on bedpan duty for a
month!'

Elizabeth smiled ruefully. 'How long will the
xi be?' she asked.

The nurse glanced at her slender wrist. 'Ten
inutes. Can I get you some tea while you're
waiting?'

Elizabeth shook her head. 'No, I'll just sit here
nd wait.'

It took longer than ten minutes for the taxi to
rrive, and Elizabeth was almost on the edge of
her wheelchair by the time it appeared. An
orderly wheeled her out through the sliding glass
doors, and she turned to wave at Nurse Jocelyn,
who watched from the desk and waved back.

The orderly stowed her wheelchair in the boot
of the car and lifted her into the back seat.
Elizabeth felt incongruous with one huge fat
plaster-covered foot and one slim one. It felt very
odd, and her skin was beginning to itch inside the
plaster, but she could only ignore it and hope the
tching would stop.

They drove quickly to Heathrow, but although
there was very little traffic on the roads her
nerves were stretched like thin wire by the time
they arrived. A porter helped her into her
wheelchair and began to wheel her across to the
V.I.P. lounge where Concorde passengers sat in
isolated splendour.

Elizabeth spotted a flower shop in the
Terminal, and went over to buy a big bouquet of
long-stemmed red roses. The porter watched her
indulgently as she clutched the flowers while she
was wheeled over to the lounge.

'Can I help you, madam?' asked a very formal
young British Airways steward, as they stopped

outside the Concorde lounge.

Elizabeth looked up at him from her wheel
chair. 'My husband is flying to New York i
thirty minutes,' she said confidently. What if sh
was wrong? What if he wasn't on this flight, bu
had already left? 'Could you check your passenge
list? I really must see him before he leaves.'

The young man adjusted his tie. 'What's th
name?'

'Mr Mark Blackthorne,' she told him, an
leaned forward avidly as he ran his pen along
computer list of names. Please let him be o
this flight, she thought, heart pounding wit
sheer anxiety.

The steward found the name and gave her
cool smile. 'Do you have any proof of identity?'

Elizabeth's heart stopped. 'Well, I've only jus
married him,' she said nervously. 'I haven't ha
time to change all my documents to his name.'

The man gave her a condescending smile. 'I'n
terribly sorry,' he said smoothly, 'but I can't le
you into the lounge unless you have proof o
identity.'

Tears pricked her eyes. To have come all thi
way for nothing! It was too much. She jus
couldn't let Mark fly off to New York thinking
she didn't love him. They would never have
another chance if that happened; his cynicisn
would shut her out of his life for ever.

'Oh please!' she begged, lower lip trembling
'It's vital that I see him!'

He shook his head. 'I'm sorry, it's agains
British Airways policy.'

Elizabeth felt her eyes water with hopelessness
'You don't understand,' she said desperately, an
held up the roses. 'I said I'd bring the roses, bu

I broke my ankle, so I couldn't put them in the window.'

The steward stared at her as if she was mad, and she blushed hotly, aware of his astonishment. But it couldn't be helped. She just had to get into that lounge before Mark left for New York. And she was ready to try anything.

'Please let me in!' Deliberately, she let the tears trickle over her cheeks instead of fighting them back. Pride was all very well, but it wouldn't bring Mark home to Carthax with her. 'Please, it's terribly important to me!'

Embarrassed, the young man stared at her, then got up, unwilling to have a scene on his hands. 'Well, I suppose I could let you in for a minute,' he said uncertainly, shifting his weight as he watched her cry. 'Don't cry any more, madam,' he whispered nervously. 'I'll let you in for a minute.'

Elizabeth sighed with relief as he took the wheelchair handles from the porter, who was watching, amused, and began to wheel her through into the V.I.P. lounge.

Her eyes scanned the lounge desperately for Mark's face. He had to be here, his name was on the list. Clutching her roses, she felt her heart pound faster as she looked towards the corner of the room.

Mark looked up, eyes blackened, just in time to see Elizabeth being wheeled towards him with her leg in plaster, smiling broadly and waving a bunch of red roses at him.

He stared for a moment, then started to rise, his lean body uncoiling gracefully. 'Elizabeth ...?' The dark blue eyes flickered over her in astonishment, seeing the tear-stained face, the hefty white lump of plaster on her leg.

Elizabeth swallowed, her heart hurting. 'I had an accident,' she said in a throaty voice. 'But I got the roses!'

He stood immobile, his face tight with emotion, his eyes flickering. 'I thought you'd decided to leave for ever,' he said deeply. 'I couldn't bear to stay anywhere near you, knowing you didn't want me.'

She gave him a tremulous smile. 'Maybe you should have your leg in plaster, too!' she said. 'Then you wouldn't be able to run away from me again!'

Slowly he reached out to take the roses from her, his hand shaking a little as he stroked the blood-red petals. 'I'm a terrible coward,' he said deeply, and his hard mouth crooked in a smile that took her breath away.

'Well,' Elizabeth looked at him through her lashes, 'you're not perfect . . . but you'll do!'

Mark bent to take her in his arms.

ANNE MATHER

Anne Mather, one of Harlequin's leading romance authors, has published more than 100 million copies worldwide, including **Wild Concerto,** a *New York Times* best-seller.

Catherine Loring was an innocent in a South American country beset by civil war. Doctor Armand Alvares was arrogant yet compassionate. They could not ignore the flame of love igniting within them...whatever the cost.

HIDDEN IN THE FLAME

Enter a uniquely exciting new world with

Harlequin American Romance ™·

Harlequin American Romances are the first romances to explore today's love relationships. These compelling novels reach into the hearts and minds of women across America... probing the most intimate moments of romance, love and desire.

You'll follow romantic heroines and irresistible men as they boldly face confusing choices. Career first, love later? Love without marriage? Long-distance relationships? All the experiences that make love real are captured in the tender, loving pages of **Harlequin American Romances.**

What makes American women so different when it comes to love? Find out with **Harlequin American Romance!**

Send for your introductory FREE book now!

Get this book FREE!

Mail to:
Harlequin Reader Service

In the U.S.
2504 West Southern Ave.
Tempe, AZ 85282

In Canada
P.O. Box 2800, Postal Station A
5170 Yonge St., Willowdale, Ont. M2N 6J3

YES! I want to be one of the first to discover
Harlequin American Romance. Send me FREE and without
obligation *Twice in a Lifetime*. If you do not hear from me after I
have examined my FREE book, please send me the 4 new
Harlequin American Romances each month as soon as they
come off the presses. I understand that I will be billed only $2.25
for each book (total $9.00). There are no shipping or handling
charges. There is no minimum number of books that I have to
purchase. In fact, I may cancel this arrangement at any time.
Twice in a Lifetime is mine to keep as a FREE gift, even if I do not
buy any additional books.   154 BPA BPGE

Name	(please print)	

Address		Apt. no.

City	State/Prov.	Zip/Postal Code

Signature (If under 18, parent or guardian must sign.)

This offer is limited to one order per household and not valid to current Harlequin
American Romance subscribers. We reserve the right to exercise discretion in
granting membership. If price changes are necessary, you will be notified.

AMR-SUB-2R

Harlequin

INDULGE IN THE PLEASURE OF SUPERB ROMANCE READING BY CHOOSING THE MOST POPULAR LOVE STORIES IN THE WORLD

Longer, more absorbing love stories for the connoisseur of romantic fiction.

Contemporary romances—uniquely North American in flavor and appeal.

An innovative series blending contemporary romance with fast-paced adventure.

and you can never have too much romance.